# Murder at Lakeland

*A Brick North Mystery*

by Augustine Meijer

عبده الغفار

ISBN-13: 978-1-7352291-0-2 (Kindle Edition)
ISBN-13: 978-1-7352291-1-9 (Paperback Edition)

Cover design by: Mark Bussemeier

A note from the author:

I grew up in the Twin Cities of Benton Harbor and Saint Joseph, Michigan. In this book I've taken the license of combining these two cities into the fictional city of LaSalle Harbor. If you're familiar with Berrien County, Michigan (renamed Douglas County in the book) or the Twin Cities, you'll note some place and road names are familiar. While I've changed some business names, other long-closed business are called by their name including "Aristo Cleaners" which was owned and operated by my maternal grandparents, Charles and Iota Kizer.

I'm proud of the community I grew up in, and while the old adage that you can never go home again is true, one can certainly do so in their memory.

# Murder at Lakeland

Monday morning found Rick North arriving late and liquored to his desk, not that there was anything unusual about either. He was tall and lean, not so much handsome as rugged; the lines on his face read like a map of the roads he'd traveled. His hair was thick, dark and wavy enough that it took more than the "little dab'll do ya," that Brylcreem advertised to keep it from falling onto his forehead. But his most striking feature was his eyes; steel blue and intense as if he were able to take in more than the average person could see.

"North!" Shouted Pete Cummings, Chief of Police for LaSalle Harbor, a manufacturing city on the shores of Lake Michigan with plenty of tourists and the problems they brought. In addition to those industries, LaSalle Harbor sat in the middle of the nation's largest fruit producing county and boasted the largest grower-to-customer wholesale market in the world. Trucks came from dozens of states in the spring and summer months to load millions of bushels of fruit; the drivers of those trucks often sought out prostitution, gambling and drugs while they were in town.

North turned toward Cummings, whose voice was still vibrating in his ears.

"Are you okay? Well, doesn't matter. Grab Tiffin when he drags his ass in here and get out to the airport. A maintenance worker just found a body in a hanger."

"Shit," North rubbed the nape of his neck, "what a way to start the week."

Cummings shook his head, "It'd start better if you weren't still drunk or hungover or whatever you are."

"I'm okay."

"Then you better call the coroner before you go and let him know that he should examine you as well as whoever that is at the airport."

North followed the smell of burned coffee to the urn in the corner of the squad room. A bit of acidic liquid trickled out of the urn, "Dammit! Can't anyone ever make coffee around here?" He slammed the cup onto the table, thought about it for a second and downed the ounce or so that had ended up in the bottom.

He looked through the dusty Venetian blinds out onto the street below. Shopkeepers were beginning to open their awnings and folks made their way into Dubois' bakery for pastry and bread for the day. The sun was already burning hot at eight o'clock in the morning and the dawn freshness was evaporating into what looked like it was going to be another scorching July day. Only a hint of a breeze entered the open window.

"Morning, Brick. You aren't thinking about getting doughnuts for me, are you?" Barry Tiffin asked as he walked up behind him. Brick was a nickname that he'd earned as a rookie when he asked to be called Rick and a sergeant added the B from his seldom-used first name, Brian. And Brick had stuck.

"Nope, just waiting for you. Don't take your hat off; we're going to the airport. Boss says they found a body out there this morning."

2

"Who the hell would go and get themselves killed at Lakeland?"

"I suppose that's what they're sending us out there to find out," North said as he crushed his worn fedora over his mop of brown hair. He stopped just long enough to pick up the phone and call dispatch to let them know where he and Tiffin were going.

Tiffin was a couple of years younger than North's thirty-four, three inches shorter and a little rounder about the midsection. It was obvious to all who took the time to notice that marriage agreed with him. They had been partners for almost three years; an arrangement that worked for both of them.

Lakeland Airport was what had become of a small Army air field installed during the Second World War for training. Twelve years later the military feel of the airport had nearly been erased with some paint and commercial signage. A cluster of buildings, including the terminal, stood on the south side of the runway, and half-dozen hangers sat on the other side. A Gulf Gas sign and pump occupied a lonely island about fifty feet from the hangers. A number of small private planes were tethered to the ground outside the two eastern-most hangers, most with canvas covers over their windows. A Northwest Orient DC-7 was being fueled near the terminal.

They spotted the black Buick Roadmaster North recognized as belonging to Doc Howard, the local surgeon who served as the Coroner for Douglas County, near one of the hangers. Alongside the Buick was the ambulance which belonged to the local mortuary. He and his partner stepped out of the blue Ford Mainline the detective squad shared.

3

"Let's find out what we've got," North said as he held his hat against the winds which blew in off of Lake Michigan. He and Tiffin stepped inside the hanger, their eyes struggling to adjust to the sudden darkness.

They found the coroner kneeling down in a corner to their right. Partially hidden by his round body was the form of a woman. As they approached, North made note of the victim. She appeared to be in her mid-twenties, her blonde hair splayed on the dirty concrete floor. She was dressed in a white blouse, which was torn at the left shoulder, blue skirt and black heels; her nylons were torn at the knees. Her body was twisted in an unnatural position as if she had crumpled to the ground more than fallen. She had applied makeup sometime before she was killed and was missing one of her false eyelashes.

"What we got here doc?" North said to the back of the sweating coroner.

Wiping his brow with his handkerchief, the coroner grunted his way to his feet. "Unknown victim, no obvious sign of trauma or coitus; been dead at least twenty-four hours; rigor's beginning to subside."

"Any idea what killed her?" the detective asked, although he already knew the answer.

"Too soon to tell."

"When will you know?"

"I'll let you know when I know, is that okay?"

"No worries doc. Was there a purse or any other belongings here?"

"Not that I've seen."

4

As they finished their exchange Tiffin approached with a lanky man dressed in blue coveralls; the name BUTCH embroidered in red letters on a white oval over his right breast. LAKELAND AIRPORT embroidered in yellow over the left.

"Brick, this is the guy that found her."

"Butch, is it?" North said as he looked first from the name patch and then down to his small black notepad.

The maintenance worker swallowed hard, his Adam's apple bobbing as he did, "Well, that's what everyone calls me, but my name's Bill er William, Henry."

"Well Bill, when did you find her?"

"When I came in this morning."

With a sigh, North changed his question, "What time did you come in and find the body?"

"Oh, about half-past seven. That's when I called you guys."

"The doc here says that she's probably been dead for a day, could she have been here since yesterday?"

"Nope, no way," the maintenance worker stood a little taller, "Id'a seen her when I was in here yesterday."

"When were you in here?"

"About three, was in here replacing a fuse in that fuse box right behind where she is and I know that I didn't step over her or anything."

"Can you explain how she got in her? Are the doors locked overnight?"

"They'd be locked if someone was using the hanger, but this one's for rent and there's nothing inside to lock up."

"Okay, thanks. I may have more questions for you later."

The maintenance man walked away and out of the hanger, Tiffin looked down at North's notepad and then his own. "Been dead a day, huh?"

North nodded. "Yep, and it doesn't look like she dropped dead here. Let's find a phone and let the chief know what we've got so far and then let's start asking if anyone saw anything."

The two detectives drove over the terminal and used a phone on the Northwest Orient Counter. North spoke loudly over an Eastern Airlines plane that made a noisy taxi over to the gate. When he'd finished reporting what they had, and hadn't found, an attractive brunette showed them to the administrator's office. She was the kind of woman that North found most appealing; tall, buxom, confident. "What's your name, should I need to call you?"

"I suppose I should give you my number too?" She said with a demure smile.

"That would be helpful, yes."

"Suzette, Yukon 5-2215." North made a note in his book.

"And your name?" her voice came out breathy.

"Rick North, but everyone calls me Brick," he replied.

"Brick? You're going to have to tell me more about that."

"Sure, doll, if you're interested, I'll tell you."

She gave him a look that told him there wouldn't be a lot of small talk the next time they met, "Here you are," and with a pause, "Brick," the word sounded suddenly dirty as she spoke it. "This is Mr. Jaeger's office." North thanked her and watched her walk away. She seemed to emphasize the heel-to-toe gait that accentuated the movement of her hips.

"You ever not on the prowl?" Tiffin whispered as they entered the office.

"Don't be jealous, Tiff."

"I just don't know what women see in you."

"And that, my friend, is because you're not a woman." At that, they turned their attention to the gentleman behind the desk. Short, balding and pockmarked, Jaeger faced away from the door, his face directly in front of an oscillating fan which sat atop the credenza. A cigarette burned in the ashtray, its smoke making a zig-zag pattern as the fan swept back and forth.

"Mr. Jaeger, we've got a few questions for you," North said as they walked in.

Jaeger turned quickly and brushed his thinning hair back with his hand. "Hot one today," he said as he motioned toward the chairs. "Won't you sit down? I'm guessing you're the police officers looking into the woman that was found. Terrible thing," and then for emphasis he added, "terrible."

North reached into his pocket and pulled out a pack of Pall Malls and his black leather note pad. He opened the pad, placed it and a pencil on the desk and lit a cigarette, with a flick his Zippo lighter clicked shut. He said, "Detectives."

"What's that?" Jaeger queried.

"We're detectives, not police officers. I'm Detective North, this is my partner, Detective Tiffin," North took a deep drag on his cigarette and let the smoke roll out of his mouth as he spoke. "What do you know about the woman that was found?"

"Know?" Jaeger said pensively, "I don't know anything about her other than she was found in hanger three."

"Who has access to the airport at night?"

"Well, everyone and no one, I guess."

"What do you mean by that?" North took another drag on his cigarette then absentmindedly pulled a piece of tobacco off his lower lip and rolled it between his fingers before flicking it onto the linoleum.

"Well, the airport closes after the last flight in the evening. Last night was the Eastern flight to Chicago. It departed at 8:00 PM. The ground crew and folks in the terminal leave about half an hour later."

"What about the guys who work in the control tower? When do they leave?"

"As soon as that flight is 20 miles over Lake Michigan and outside our air space. Probably within 15 minutes."

"So, the airport is locked down?" Tiffin threw out while North took another pull on his cigarette.

"Well, the buildings are locked, but there's no way to keep people from coming onto the grounds."

North tucked the cigarette into the corner of his mouth and pick up the pencil and pad, "Do planes come in overnight?"

"Well, sure some private pilots will fly in at odd hours, but they file a flight plan so we know when they're supposed to arrive."

Tiffin's face took on a frustrated appearance, "Okay, here's what I'm hearing. Buildings are locked, except of course hanger three which wasn't. Grounds are open so anyone could drive in here and dump a body or maybe fly in, drop off the body and fly out."

"Who knew the hanger would be unlocked?" North jumped in, pulling the Pall Mall away from his lip, the paper sticking a bit.

Jaeger's head pivoted from Tiffin to North, "Sorry, what's that?"

"Who would know that hanger three wouldn't be locked? It can't be a coincidence that someone had a body to dump and just happened to come to the airport and just happened to find an unlocked hanger."

Jaeger looked between the two detectives as he tried to come up with an answer. "I guess I don't know. It's not that we have an empty hanger all that often."

"Your man Bill Henry would know, right? He's the one that left it unlocked after he'd done some electrical work out there." North remarked while giving the airport manager a very direct look. "Other than him, who would know?"

"Well, I guess I would." Jaeger offered nervously.

"Anyone else, Mr. Jaeger, anyone you can think of?"

"Former employees."

"How about the ground crews, tower personnel and the folks working in the terminal?" Tiffin asked.

"No, I wouldn't think so. Their work doesn't take them to the hangers."

North leaned forward as a thought popped into mind, "what about the private pilots? What would keep them from looking around? They park out toward the hangers and walk to their planes, don't they?"

"I guess, sure that's possible."

"Can you get me the names of those who own the planes that are parked out there right now?"

"Give me a minute, I'll look that up."

Jaeger stepped out and North took a moment to look more deeply at the office. The green metal desk and credenza obviously had been left when Army sold the property, same with the file cabinet. There was a framed photo of two boys that was taken on the shore of Lake Michigan; LaSalle Harbor's twin lighthouses visible in the background. A framed sectional aeronautical chart of the area was above the credenza. On the desk was a lamp, its fluorescent bulb flickering, a telephone, some paperwork, an amber-colored ashtray overflowing with cigarette butts, and a wooden block with the name "Harold Jaeger" roughly burned into it.

"One of the kids probably made that," North thought to himself.

"Here it is," Jaeger said as he walked in and handed North a manifest.

"There are nine planes listed here."

"That's right," Jaeger said as he lit another cigarette, "nine planes all owned by folks here…"

"No, not right," North interrupted, "there are ten planes out there."

"That can't be!" Jaeger said in a defensive and loud manner, "Every plane is accounted for."

"Not this time," Tiffin piped in, "maybe we should compare your manifest with the planes on the field."

With the paperwork in hand, he and North drove back over to the hangers. They compared the tail numbers on each plane with the manifest. The last plane in the line, one of the few without a tarp over the windows, was not listed.

"Here's one that doesn't belong," Tiffin said over the roar of a commercial flight taking off, "tail number N-2480-P."

North looked into the cockpit of the plane, "nothing unusual that I can see. You call this in while I go ask Mr. Jaeger how this bird got here without being on his manifest."

Back in the terminal, Tiffin went over to the counter where they'd used the phone earlier, North walked back to the airport manager's office.

"Well, Mr. Jaeger, there's a plane out there that doesn't belong. If I give you the tail number can you tell me who it belongs to?"

Jaeger shifted uncomfortably in his chair, "It'll take some time, but sure. What's the number?"

"November Two Four Eight Zero Papa." Brick read from his pad.

"Okay, I'll call the Civil Aeronautics Board and see who it's registered to."

"How long will it take?" North said the impatience could be heard in his voice.

"It's the government. It could be 5 minutes or it could be tomorrow. Depends."

"You tell them it's a police matter and you need to know as quickly as possible, then call me." North pushed a business card across the desk.

"Oh, yes, certainly." Jaeger slid the card into the center desk drawer.

North found Tiffin sitting in the terminal flicking cigarette ashes into a standing ashtray by the seats. With his legs crossed, a hole the size of a half dollar was visible in the sole of the brown wingtips he wore.

"Geez, Tiff," North said, "Why don't you get those things resoled?"

"I don't know, Brick. Same reason I don't do a lot of things. Two kids, mortgage, car payment, wife wants an automatic washing machine. Got a bunch of stuff that comes before taking care of my shoes."

"I'll loan you the two bucks to get those fixed."

"Thanks, but we're getting by."

"I used to think I'd be happier if I settled down and got married. Thanks for talking me out of it." North said with a smile. "Come on, let's get back downtown and start working with what we've got."

North parallel parked the Ford with practiced hand in front of the Public Safety Building which housed both the Police and Fire Departments. The concrete steps leading up to the front doors were worn from thousands of feet over the years. The doors themselves were heavy brass, mostly weathered to a dark brown except for the handles which glowed like gold from constantly being touched. Inside the smell of paper and stale coffee mixed with a tinge of cleaning solution assaulted the nostrils. The sound of high heels against terrazzo tile mimicked the typewriters that clicked incessantly.

As they passed the dispatch office a voice called out, "Hey, Brick. How're you doing?" It was Sylvia, one of a dozen women who fielded phone calls and transferred them to the appropriate party.

"I'm okay, Syl, how about you?" Sylvia wasn't exactly North's type; a petite blonde, but she was round in all the right places and while not a looker, was attractive and always eager for a drink after work. North knew that she was looking to settle down, and she knew that he wasn't. But somehow it worked for them and they'd end up at the Trophy Room down the street for a drink and a burger a few times a month. Occasionally they'd end up back at his room at the old Swanson Hotel.

"If you're not doing anything later, I thought maybe we could…"

"I've pulled the murder case at the airport, I don't know if I'll be free tonight or not."

"Well, if you'd like maybe I could bring something up to your room tonight if you're too tired to go out," she said, her head cocked slightly to the side and a hint of a smile on her lips.

"Yeah sure, maybe we could do that. I'll let you know."

Tiffin turned from the elevator down the hall, "You coming or not?"

Toward his partner, he said, "I'll catch up with you in a minute." Toward Sylvia, he said in a lower voice, "Bring your toothbrush."

Blushing she replied, "I always do."

With long strides, North walked the corridor and, hesitating at the elevator for a moment, turned the corner and took the stairs instead.

"North!" Chief Cummings called from his office, "Get in here." He walked into the cramped office, much of the usable space taken up by the large oak desk and file cabinets that lined two of the walls. The Chief pointed toward one of the green leather-covered chairs indicating for North to sit, "Tiffin was just catching me up about the girl, the airplane that doesn't belong, and that's all you've got for a morning's worth of work."

"And the hanger that wasn't locked and that someone would have had to know that they could get in and out unseen. So, we've got a little more than that, but nothing much yet to go on. The airport manager..."

"I don't need the details; just get to work on figuring this out."

"On it, Chief," Tiffin nodded toward Cummings whose former red hair had begun to succumb to grey. The bags under Cummings eyes revealed the responsibility he bore.

Tiffin and North walked back into the squad room, the early afternoon sun was almost straight overhead, and not a shadow could be seen on the street below them. They made a couple of phone calls, Tiffin to his wife, North to the coroner. "Doc Howard hasn't had time to start the autopsy yet; says he might not get to it until tomorrow. I think I'm in need of some lunch," North said as he grabbed his hat and walked toward the stairwell. "I'm right behind you," Tiffin added.

On the door of the Trophy Room was a weather-beaten sign proclaiming Air Conditioned; North was glad for it. The sweatband inside his hat was saturated as was his shirt collar. Tossing the hat and his jacket onto one of the chairs at the table he and Tiffin grabbed, he plopped down on his chair which forced the barrel of his .38 into the chair and the shoulder holster uncomfortably into his side. He readjusted the holster and leaned back in the chair, listening to it creak as he rocked on the chair's back two legs.

North motioned for the waitress who sauntered over, "Hey Brick, hey Tiff," she said in a raspy voice that echoed the years of cigarettes she'd smoked, "what'll it be fellas?"

"A beer and a bump for me."

"I'll have a beer and have Charlie drop a burger on the grill for me," added Tiffin. "You not eating, Brick?" he said toward his partner.

"Nah, food doesn't sound good."

Two beers and a shot of whiskey appeared on their table. Without ceremony, North threw the shot back and chased it with some beer. Tiffin took a sip of the cold brew and sat back, watching the sweat on the glass ripple toward the paper Blatz coaster it sat on.

"So what'ya thinking, Brick?" He said, more out of boredom than real interest.

"I'm thinking there's something bigger going on here than what we see so far. I'm thinking that the girl doesn't belong here, the plane doesn't belong here, and who the hell would fly to LaSalle Harbor to dump a body, and if you did, why wouldn't you fly away. I'm thinking I need another whiskey," he said as he held the empty shot glass over his head and caught the waitress's eye.

"Right away," the waitress called over her shoulder as she walked toward the old oak bar which ran the length of the building. Brick gave her a quick smile, his left eye blinking a bit as he did.

"Maybe we should get a search warrant to go through the plane?" Tiffin said as the waitress, a big old friendly gal with a white apron tied about her waist, sat the whiskey down and took away the other shot glass.

North took a sip of his beer and lit a cigarette. He took a deep pull on the Pall Mall and leaned in over the table, "That'll take too long. Let's just go have a better look at the plane."

The burger and a bottle of ketchup were put on the table in front of Tiffin. "Anything else, boys?" the waitress asked as she picked up the now empty shot glass and wiped up the condensation on the table with a rag. North contemplated another shot and decided against it. He

16

sipped at his beer and spent the time Tiffin used to eat watching the other patrons of the bar. Most of them were regulars. One man sat alone at a table in the corner. He didn't seem to be paying any attention to the beer in front of him but did seem to be looking toward the detectives when North looked his way. As Tiffin wiped his chin and crumpled the paper napkin into a wad, North crushed his cigarette out and motioned again to the waitress.

"Put it on my tab Roxy," North said as he handed her a shiny Franklin half dollar for a tip. "I can pay for my lunch," Tiffin argued. "Hell Tiff, you can't afford to get your shoes fixed." With that, he stood, adjusted the holster, slipped his suit jacket over it and crushed the fedora onto his head. "See ya, Roxy," he called over his shoulder as they walked into the sweltering afternoon.

Once back to the airport they drove immediately out to the line of planes. Two that had been there this morning were gone. The suspicious plane was still where it had been. Tiffin ducked under the wing and looked into the cockpit. "Door's locked, but looks pretty clean in here," he called back to North who was looking at a luggage compartment door on the side of the plane.

"If you had a dead girl, would you lift her to get her in there," he said motioning toward the cockpit with his chin, "or would you slide her in back here?" Tiffin walked back to North as North tugged on the handle.

"Fabric over a metal frame, I should be able to jimmy the door open," and with a tug that rocked the plane, the door opened revealing a cramped compartment that ran behind the rear seat. "That look big enough to put a body?"

Tiffin shown his flashlight into the space, "I wouldn't want to be back there, but sure, I think you could get a body in here."

"Let me see that light," North said as he pushed his head and a shoulder into the compartment. After a moment he said, "Look what I got," as he backed out and held a false eyelash up for Tiffin to see. "I think we can say that this is definitely how she got here. Let's go over and see if Jaeger has gotten anything on who this bird might belong to."

The July sun was beating down and the heat in the car's interior took their breath away as they climbed into the Ford. North could feel the sweat roll between his shoulder blades. He turned the wheel and drove quickly to the terminal building. Air rushed through the vent and into the cabin making it slightly more tolerable.

He found a bit of shade under an awning where the luggage truck would normally park and they walked back inside. "Hey Brick," the brunette from this morning called out from behind the counter, "you back to see me?" she added with a smile.

"Yeah doll, right after I see your boss. He in?"

"He's in, eating at his desk like every day."

The two detectives made their way into the non-public space of the terminal. A large fan moved air down the corridor, the thrum not unlike the planes that moved around outside. "Mr. Jaeger?" Tiffin, who'd reached the door first, called in.

Jaeger seemed edgy, "Oh, come on in. Just got a call back from the CAB, November Two Four Eight Zero Papa," he said as he read from his handwritten notes, "a 1953 Piper Tri-Pacer is registered to a Dr. Herbert Dalander out of Grand Rapids."

"What's Grand Rapids, 100 – 120 miles?" North asked, more to himself as he recorded the information into his note pad.

"By air, probably about 90," Jaeger offered.

Tiffin looked between North and the airport manager. "How long would it take someone in that plane to fly from there to here?"

"With a tailwind, maybe an hour, hour and a quarter depending on how much the pilot was pushing it."

North pushed the black leather note pad back into his pocket. "I guess that's all we need right now, thank you."

"Oh, glad to help," Jaeger said as he unwrapped the waxed paper from around his sandwich. "Let me know what else I can do for you."

Back downtown North stepped into the switchboard. "Hey, Syl, can you make a call for me?"

"Sure, Brick. Who am I calling?"

"Call the Grand Rapids P.D., I'm looking to see what they know about a Dr. Herbert Dalander."

"I'll ring it upstairs to you as soon as I connect." Then in a lower voice, "I'm looking forward to tonight." North smiled and headed toward the elevator.

Tiffin had grabbed the mail out of the pigeon hole on the way up. "Got something for you," he said as he handed an envelope to North. "Looks official," he added.

"Yeah, it's from the Attorney General's office. The dumb asses at the State are still bothered about that kid who fell down the stairs on his way to booking back in April. They want to talk to me about it."

"Again," Tiffin looked perplexed. "I thought that was settled."

"I did too, but I guess his daddy is some bigwig who has the ear of someone in Lansing."

"Well, I saw you grab his back trying to keep him from falling."

"If he hadn't been such a smart ass, he probably wouldn't have tripped."

Tiffin nodded. North put his fedora onto the top of the coat rack and hung his wrinkled brown suit coat on the back of his chair. He tossed the unopened envelope on the corner of the desk. Tiffin threw his jacket onto a hook on the coat rack and rolled up his sleeves, revealing a Navy tattoo on his right forearm. The phone rang and North beat Tiffin to it.

"North," he said into the receiver. "Okay, let me talk to them." He put his hand over the mouthpiece, "It's the Grand Rapids police, I guess the good doctor is missing." Then back into the phone, "This is Detective North…"

## Chapter 2

Light from the street below filtered into North's room at the Swanson Hotel. The ancient wallpaper had taken on a yellow tinge from years of nicotine. An uncorked bottle of Old Quaker bourbon and two glasses sat on the small table along with his badge, keys and wallet. North's worn brown leather holster hung over the back of the chair, the .38 within reach of the bed should it be needed.

"Does it hurt?" Sylvia asked as she traced the edge of the scar on North's right torso with her fingertip.

"Nah," he replied, "I don't notice it anymore." Her head rested upon his chest and in the dim light he could make out the curve of her hip. His rough hand felt somehow foreign against her smooth skin as he slid it down her side and over that curve, and let it rest against her thigh.

"You've never told me how you got that," she said softly as if her words would disturb the quiet moment.

"It doesn't matter doll," he said while his mind turned itself back to that bloody night at Monte Cassino when a squadron of B-17 Flying Fortresses destroyed the ancient abbey, which instead of housing a German artillery observation post had actually sheltered civilians from the village. A Nazi infantry unit used the chaos of falling bombs and dying civilians to approach North's unit from the rear and wreak havoc. A bullet had ripped through his right-side carrying part of a rib with it. For just a moment the smell of blood and cordite and the screams of women and children filled his senses. Sylvia's touch brought him back to his room. "It's just a reminder of friends I lost, that's all," he lied as she laid her head back upon his chest.

After Sylvia had fallen asleep, North slipped into his clothes and, more out of habit than anything, flipped the cylinder of his service revolver open and checked that all six rounds were there. He quietly closed it and slipped it into the holster under his right arm. Lighting a cigarette, he stepped out of the room into the hall. He gave a quick glance toward Sylvia curled up on her side and looking catlike under the cotton chenille bedspread as he pulled the door shut.

Once outside he did what he so often did at night, he walked the sleeping streets and let his mind race through the thoughts of the day and the images of a war now twelve years in the past. Just a block off of Main Street the houses of LaSalle Harbor's factory workers and shopkeepers were arranged in a neat grid. In most neighborhoods each house looked like every other house with the exception of trim and color. A single street light cast a yellow glow at every intersection and very few of the houses had any lights on inside.

He'd walked for a while when he thought he heard a footstep behind him. He stopped and took a look over his shoulder but didn't see anything. Alert, the thoughts he'd been pondering now pushed away, he began walking again, this time a little faster. Stopping suddenly, he distinctly heard footfalls stutter to a stop. North raced around a corner and quickly tucked himself behind a Rhododendron which stood next to a clapboarded house. He pulled the revolver from under his jacket and waited for whoever it was that was following him. Within seconds the frame of a large man lurched into view. The man stopped and looked around. In the orb of the streetlight, North thought he recognized him as the man from the Trophy Room earlier that afternoon. The large man looked around for a moment, seemed to make a decision and began to quickly walk down the street to the right, disappearing into the darkness.

North retraced his steps keeping an eye out for the man who had been followed him. Reholstering his gun he returned to the Swanson and made his way back to his third-floor room. The smell of baking bread wafted up the street from the Dubois and into his open window. Sylvia yawned and stretched as he entered. "What time is it?" she asked in a sleepy voice.

"About four," he said quietly.

"I should think about getting home before I have to get to work," she added as she slipped out from under the bedding. In the dim light of the room, North took in her nakedness as she gathered up her clothes. She slipped into her lingerie and, sitting on the edge of the bed, rolled the nylons up her legs, snapping the clasps hanging from the garter belt to the tops of the hose. She finished dressing and, grabbing her purse, walked out of the room to the common bathroom at the end of the hall. A few minutes later she returned and with a kiss on the cheek left North to his thoughts. He heard her car start on the street below and sat back on the bed hoping that sleep would come.

At some point it did because he woke with a start as the morning sun struck him fully on the face. He looked at his watch which read a quarter past seven. He rolled off the bed and after coming back from the bathroom, pulled the bedding up and straightened the room. He looked at the bottle of Old Quaker on the table and fought the urge to take a nip. He reinserted the cork instead and finished getting dressed.

On the street, he walked to the Fifth Wheel Café and wolfed down a plate of bacon and eggs and washed it down with a cup of coffee. "Did I eat yesterday?" he thought to himself as he dropped a dollar onto the counter, "Keep the change," he said to the waitress as he walked toward the screen door. On the street he found himself looking into the shop windows trying to see if the big man was following him. He didn't see him and began to think himself paranoid as he made his way up the steps of the Safety Building. Tiffin was already at his desk when he got upstairs.

"Jesus, Brick," he said as North tossed his hat onto the coat rack, "you look like hell. Don't you ever sleep?"

"I slept enough."

"I got two screaming kids at home and I get more sleep than you," Tiffin threw out as Chief Cummings walked into the squad room.

"Tiffin, North, grab a car, you're going to Grand Rapids. I want you to liaison with the Grand Rapids PD, let's see what you can find out about this missing doctor."

"Okay, chief," North said as Tiffin picked up the phone to explain to his wife why he wouldn't be at their son's little league game that afternoon.

"Oh, North," the chief looked directly at him, "grab a shave before you go. You look like shit."

Ignoring the chief's request, he and Tiffin grabbed the keys to the squad's Ford and went down to the motor pool. They filled up at the city yard and headed out to the highway. Two and a half hours later they arrived in Grand Rapids covered in sweat and a thin layer of dust that blew in through the windows as they drove.

The two stopped in a diner, checked out the plumbing and washed up before grabbing a sandwich and a cup of coffee. North drank his black, Tiffin added milk and a liberal amount of sugar.

They made their way to the city's Police Building. Parking around the corner, Tiffin dropped a dime into the parking meter. They waiting for a trolley to pass before crossing into the building which smelled exactly the same as the one they left in LaSalle Harbor. Walking up to an elevated counter where an older sergeant looked down at them, North said, "We're out of the LaSalle Harbor Police Department and are here to talk to your detectives about a missing doctor."

"Yeah, Doc Dalander is up and gone. I heard his plane was found down in your parts," the sergeant said as he directed the two down the hall. Once inside the squad room, they were met by their counterpart, who introduced himself as Ed Newkirk. Newkirk was around fifty, solidly built with wide shoulders and a growing middle-age girth. "So, you boys want to know why our doctor's plane is at your airport and why he isn't here. Does that about sum it up?" Newkirk asked. "Shame you haven't got a working telephone down in the boonies; it would have saved you a long drive," he added sarcastically.

"Hell, Newkirk," North threw back, "We wanted to see what a big city asshole looks like. Guess we can go home now, Tiff," he said to his partner.

Newkirk let out a laugh that filled the room, "Sit down let me tell you what I know about Doc and Mrs. Dalander." The two pulled up chairs to Newkirk's worn desk which was covered with stacks of paper and file folders.

"Dalander practices general medicine on the north side. Nothing unusual about his practice as far as I can tell. He's a Swede, moved to the States after the war. His missus is a local gal; high society type, the kind that likes to be noticed."

"What does Dalander look like?" North asked as he wrote in his pad.

"Mid-fifties, six-foot, typical Swede with blonde hair and blue eyes. Very pale completion and a scar on his right cheek."

"Plane seems like a rather large investment, even for a doctor," Tiffin said, making a statement more than a question. "Does he come from money?"

"No. He arrived here after the war with little more than a medical degree and the clothes on his back."

North looked up from his pad, "Then Mrs. Dalander comes from a well-to-do family."

"Joan? No, her father was a farmer."

"Doctors make more than detectives, but unless they're some fancy surgeon, they don't make that much. Where's he getting the money to buy a plane?" North asked.

"Well, hadn't thought much about it. I can tell you that they've got a nice house up in the Heritage Hills neighborhood." Newkirk added.

"You wanna take a drive up there Newkirk?"

"Sure. Let me get my hat. I'll drive," adding, "I know the area better than you guys who just fell off the hay wagon."

The three of them walked out the backdoor of the building and onto a gravel parking lot. A black Chevy Biscayne sat in the shade of the building. Newkirk and North took the front seat, Tiffin climbed into the back. Once the car was started Newkirk reached under the dash and turned on the Motorola two-way radio. He waited a minute for the tubes to warm up, then keyed the microphone. "Delta 1-2, Delta 1-2 to P.D." "P.D. Delta 1-2, go ahead," the disembodied voice of a female answered, "Delta 1-2, I'm heading to the home of Doc Dalander in Heritage Hills."

"Affirmative, Delta 1-2."

Newkirk smiled at his guests, "Two-way radio, boys. Bet you ain't got that down in the sticks."

"Holy shit, Newkirk," North blustered, "we're still using smoke signals." The three of them laughed as Newkirk turned the car onto the main road which they followed several miles out of town.

To North's eye, the Dalander home was vulgar and pretentious. From the looks of it, the house was probably built in the 1890s and added to until it was overelaborate with gingerbread trim and a turret that seemed to serve no purpose but to be there. "Kind of reminds me of the pictures of that church in Red Square that I've seen," Tiffin said to North over the seat.

Newkirk parked the car and they walked up the steps onto a large porch that wrapped around the front of the house. He twisted the doorbell and waited. A few moments later a woman came to the door. "Mrs. Dalander?" North asked. "Oh my, no," the woman replied, "I'm Mrs. Johnson, the maid. Mrs. Dalander is at the club. It's her bridge day."

"The club?" North queried.

"The River Valley Country Club," Newkirk offered.

"Every Tuesday afternoon Mrs. Dalander plays bridge at the club." the maid said. "Are you with the police?"

North smiled to himself. Was it their cheap suits, the black car with no trim, or their general demeanor that gave them away? "Yes ma'am. I'm Detective North and this is Detective Tiffin and Detective Newkirk. We're making inquiry into Doctor Dalander's disappearance."

"Disappearance?" Mrs. Johnson looked aghast. "The doctor hasn't disappeared. He's just on one of his trips."

"One of his trips?" Tiffin asked before the other two could.

"Oh, he travels all over. He helps sick people all over the state."

"A regular Albert Schweitzer, is he?" North's sarcasm brimmed over.

"No need for that Detective," Newkirk said to North. Then to the maid, "Thank you for your help."

Back in the Chevy Newkirk radioed the police department regarding their change of venue, turned the car onto the main road and headed toward the Grand River and the River Valley Country Club. Once there he parked in front of the white two-story clubhouse, the negro doorman ran towards him, "Excuse me, sir," he said in a deferential manner, "but you cannot park here." Newkirk flashed the badge on his belt. The doorman backed away saying softly, "Oh, yes sir, yes sir."

In the foyer between two staircases that curved up to the second floor was an information desk; a blonde debutant in a blue blazer and white pleated skirt stood behind it. "Gentlemen?" she said in a voice that was neither too loud nor too quiet.

"We're here to see Mrs. Dalander," North said as he looked directly into her eyes; eyes that seemed vacant.

"Mrs. Dalander is in the card room on the second floor. Would you like me to take you there?" The detectives nodded and she led them up the right staircase and turned into a large warmly appointed room. North took in the room; the walls were paneled in oak, the carpet and curtains were scarlet, over the fireplace was a prominent painting of an older man standing in front of a white horse. Five card tables were arranged in the center of the room under the chandelier, each table had four chairs and each chair was occupied by a woman wearing white gloves and a small hat, holding cards. "Mrs. Dalander is there on the right," the deb said as she politely pointed with her head toward a middle-aged woman whose dark hair was showing the first signs of silver.

"Mrs. Joan Dalander? I'm detective Newkirk from the Grand Rapids Police Department. She and the other three women at the table lowered their cards, "Is there a place we can speak privately?" Mrs. Dalander excused herself from the table promising to be right back and walked the detectives into a smaller room off to the side.

"You've found Herbert?" she asked with trepidation. "No," Newkirk said looking toward the other two detectives, "these men are with the LaSalle Harbor police department."

"LaSalle Harbor, why would they be here?"

North answered, "Mrs. Dalander, your husband's plane was found at the Lakeland Airport in LaSalle Harbor yesterday."

"That's not possible," she remarked, "he was on his way to Chicago, why would his plane be in LaSalle Harbor?"

"That's what we're trying to figure out, Mrs. Dalander," Tiffin responded. "When did you last see your husband?"

"About two o'clock on Sunday when he left for the airport. He always calls when he gets into Meigs Field and he didn't. He should have been there by dinner time. When I didn't hear from him, I called the police."

"Your maid said that your husband often flew to provide medical assistance around the state, is that true?" North requested.

"Well, yes he does, but we don't always tell the staff where he's going. Frankly, it's none of their business."

"Why was he going to Chicago, Mrs. Dalander?" North asked.

"I'm not sure that's relevant," she said defensively. "You need to find out where he is and not why was he going to Chicago."

"Ma'am, we need to track down all the leads." North said, adding, "Let me ask you this, and know that at this time I can't tell you why I'm asking, but would your husband have been traveling with a woman, maybe mid-twenties with blonde hair?"

"Just what are you implying?!" she said, her voice loud enough that the conversation in the card room came to an abrupt halt.

"I'm not implying anything and I don't know if there's any connection whatsoever. I just wanted to know if he had a traveling companion on his trip to Chicago. That's all."

"That's not what you asked. You asked if my husband was traveling with a woman. The answer is no. The answer to your question about a traveling companion is also no. He was going to Chicago to give a lecture at the University Medical School and was due to come home last night."

"Thank you, Mrs. Dalander. We'll let you know as soon as we have any information regarding your husband's whereabouts," the Grand Rapids detective said as he motioned for the former farmer's daughter to return to the card room.

As they came back down from the second floor North took in the debutant behind the counter. Probably about nineteen, but instead of a normal bouncy young woman she seemed vacuous. He continued to look at her as they came around the counter and she seemed unperturbed that a middle-aged man was literally staring at her. She offered no expression of displeasure at his glare, or for that matter, any expression whatsoever.

Back in the car Newkirk again radioed the police department. "You know something, Brick," Tiffin said from the backseat, "something doesn't sit right with the missus back there. She's more defensive than she is concerned."

"Yeah, I'm feeling a little uneasy about her story too," North said as Newkirk steered the Chevy back toward the Police Station.

Once there Newkirk asked the switchboard to connect him to the Dean of the University of Chicago's medical school. It took about ten minutes before the phone rang back. "Newkirk," he said as he picked up the phone, "hold for Dr. Othello Eckstein," the operator's voice said before there was a click, "Go ahead," she said. "Dr. Eckstein? This is

Detective Edward Newkirk from the Grand Rapids Michigan Police Department. Sir, I'm trying to verify that Dr. Herbert Dalander was scheduled to lecture at the medical school yesterday."

"Who?" Eckstein said.

"Dr. Herbert Dalander from Grand Rapids, Michigan," Newkirk repeated.

"Not only was he not scheduled to lecture, but I also have no idea who he is."

"I'm so sorry to have bothered you, Doctor. Good day."

"Well boys," Newkirk said as he hung up the phone, "the University has never heard of our Dr. Dalander, so it looks like he may have fibbed a little bit to his wife."

"Or his wife is lying to us," North added. "The airport manager back home said that pilots have to file a flight plan. Can we check with the airport up here and see where he told them he was going?" Newkirk picked up the receiver and asked the switchboard to call the airport. After hanging up with the airport office he turned to his counterparts, "Dalander was bound for Chicago. According to the airport, he's flown there twice a month for the past several years."

North and Tiffin exchanged glances. Tiffin said what everyone else was thinking, "If he isn't lecturing at the University of Chicago, and he isn't off curing the sick in Western Michigan, just what the hell is he doing?"

"And there's the mystery," Newkirk said as he leaned back in the old wooden swivel chair at his desk. "You boys staying the night? I know a good bar where I could show you how we operate in the big city."

"Nah," North said without having to look at his partner, "I think the boonies are calling us." They shook hands and promised to keep each other up on the investigation.

The two stopped in at the same diner they had visited earlier and took turns at the payphone. Tiffin called his wife and North the chief before they gassed up the car and headed back to LaSalle Harbor. "We aren't any further ahead than we were yesterday," Tiffin said as he steered onto the US Highway that was the most direct route home. "No," agreed North, "if anything we've added to the problem."

He and Tiffin compared notes, "Girl dead. Who is she?"

"Don't know."

"Was she brought in on Dalander's plane?"

"Looks like it."

"Where's Dalander?"

"Don't know."

"Why's he going to Chicago so much?"

"Don't know."

"Where's a small-time doc get enough money for a private plane, a fancy house, and a country club membership?"

The two looked at each other for a moment. North finally broke the silence, "If we find that out the rest of this will probably fall into place."

"You're probably right, Brick," Tiffin added over the noise of the tires on the asphalt. "But, we're still no further ahead and the chief will probably be on our asses for wasting a day."

"Tiff," North replied with a touch of humor in his voice, "remember, he asked us to go to Grand Rapids. If there's shit to pay, it's on his tab, not ours."

By nine o'clock the Ford was back at the motor pool, Tiffin was in his car and on his way out to the suburbs and North was walking Main on his way to the Swanson. He'd just passed from the glow of a street light into darkness when he was hit from behind.

The weight of the blow rocked him forward and his face and shoulder struck the brick wall of an alley. He turned and swung toward his assailant, landing a punch before a powerful blow landed in the small of his back, sending him to his knees. He rolled onto his back and brought his shoes into the midriff of a big man who was hovering over him. With a grunt, the big man staggered back and North rolled to his hands and knees in an effort to regain his footing. A large booted foot kicked him in the ribs and he fell onto the brick alleyway. The boot swung twice more, each time with a solid crunch. North laid there for a moment with the wind knocked out of him. He started reaching for the .38 under his arm when the boot came down between his shoulder blades holding him in down. "The boss says you can either back off or you can be dead. Don't matter to me which you choose. Just know that I'll be keeping an eye on you and that little whore you're sleeping with." The boot lifted off North's back and swung hitting him in the jaw and sending him into darkness.

A bright light and sal volatile under his nose brought him back to consciousness. He tried to raise himself from the cot he was on but fell back from the pain in his rib cage and his jaw. "Steady, Brick," Doc Howard's voice came from what seemed like the next county, "just lay back and let's get a better look at you."

"It was the guy from the bar," North tossed out.

"Right now, it doesn't matter if it was the Burlington Northern. At the moment we've got to make sure you're all right."

"I'm fine, Doc. Eisenhower's the President, it's 1957, my name is Rick North and your name is Howard. Now let me get up."

"You've got at least two broken ribs and a probable concussion, not to mention some deep tissue contusions, a couple of lacerations and I think you broke a couple of knuckles."

"Another day at the beach, Doc. Just let me get back to my room and I'll be fine."

"I can't leave you alone, I don't know if you have any more serious injuries. The patrolmen brought you to my office; I should take you to the hospital."

"Fuck that," North grunted as he pushed himself off the cot. "You want to keep an eye on me, you can come to the Swanson with me. Otherwise, leave me the hell alone." He found his shirt, holster and jacket folded on a chair in the corner and with some effort, he pulled them on. "Where's my hat?" he said toward Doc Howard.

"Didn't come in with you," the doctor offered.

"Shit, I get the crap kicked out of me and I lose my hat? What's wrong with this world? Drive me home and let's stop and see if we can find it."

"First, let's bind those ribs."

North gave him an annoyed look, "Do what you need to do and help me find my hat."

Howard did just that. They stopped where North figured he was assaulted and sure enough, his old brown Bradmore sat in the shadows. North stepped out of the Buick and with not a little effort stooped down and grabbed the hat and pushed it over his disheveled hair. The two flights of stairs up to his room took some determination to climb. He turned the key and he and Doc Howard entered. He plopped down in the chair and grabbed the bottle of bourbon. With an effort, he pulled the cork and sucked at least one shot from the bottle. After doing so he held it toward the doctor.

"I'll pass," the doctor said. "Can I help get you out of your clothes and into bed?"

North gave a rough laugh, "You ain't my type," he said.

"Why don't you lay down and I'll just sit here." North laid back on the bed and within minutes was asleep. The doctor took the Gideon Bible from the nightstand. He flipped it open to the Gospel of John and read the first verse he saw, "sin no more lest a worse thing come unto thee." "How appropriate, how very fucking appropriate," he said to himself.

## Chapter 3

With a little struggle, North got out of bed. Doc Howard had wrapped his ribs tightly and his jaw didn't hurt too badly if he didn't open it too wide. He downed a shot of bourbon before reaching to pull on a t-shirt.

The mirror above the sink in his room showed the damage as North took a moment to look himself over. He had a dark bruise on his left jaw and cheek. A smaller bruise was on the right side of his forehead where it and the alley wall had met. He washed his face in cold water, which he thought would feel better than warm, lathered up and shaved.

He managed to get his holster on and a suit jacket over the top of everything. On the way out of the Swanson, he left some clothes at the front desk to be cleaned. "You okay, Mr. North?" the desk clerk asked with concern.

"Oh, I'm fine, Mike, just fine." There were times that sarcasm was the only language North spoke, this was one of them.

He thought for a moment of dropping into the Fifth Wheel for a cup of coffee but didn't want to be the object of anyone's stares. That and he wanted to get to the office and try to figure out who had roughed him up; he needed to return the favor in all due haste.

He passed by the telephone room and took the elevator to the second floor. "Hey Brick," Tiffin said in a conciliatory tone, "you okay?"

"Never better," North grunted in reply, "and why the fuck you talking like I'm retarded? I've had broken ribs before."

"Well, it's not every day that you do."

"And it's not every day that someone tries to keep me from doing my job. Anything on our dead girl or about Dalander?"

"Not yet."

"I'm gonna get a cup o' joe then I'm going to find out who that big guy is and who he's working for."

"There's coffee in the urn," Tiffin added, "you want me to get you a cup?"

"Nah, I think I can handle it. But maybe you should call the ambulance and have them waiting."

After a quick cup of coffee, the two detectives walked over to the Trophy Room. Knowing that it wouldn't be open yet, they went around to the alley entrance. Roxy was in the kitchen peeling hardboiled eggs before dropping them into a large jug of purple pickling solution. "Hey Brick, Tiff, what's up?"

"Wanted to ask you and Charlie about a customer you had in here Monday at lunchtime. Do you remember the big guy who was sitting by himself in the corner?"

"Hard to forget him, he nursed that beer for over an hour and left me a dime for a tip."

"Did you talk to him? Did he mention where he was from or anything that might help us figure out who he is?" North said through his aching jaw.

"He wasn't the talkative type if you know what I mean," the old waitress said. "But he did complain that beer was cheaper in Chicago."

"Anything else you can remember about him?" Tiffin asked.

"I don't know. He was nervous like. Sort of kept looking at the door and eyeing the other customers when they came in. He must have smoked a pack of cigarettes while he sat there. I had to bring him a clean ashtray at one point."

"Well, thanks, Roxy. If you think of anything else give me a call, will you?" North said as he and Tiffin made their way back to the alley door.

"You know what?" Roxy called after them. "He did leave an empty matchbook on the table when he left. I thought it was strange because it was from a motor court in Niles and I thought why would he drive 20 miles for a beer? Know what I mean?"

North grabbed his notebook. "You remember what motor court it was from?"

"Tall Pines, I think. Yeah, that's it, Tall Pines. I remember because of the trees on the matchbook."

"Roxy, I'd kiss you if Charlie wouldn't get jealous," North said with a smile that ached.

"I won't tell him," the big gal said with a laugh.

North and Tiffin walked back to the Safety Building and checked the Ford Mainline out of the motor pool. "You drive," North said as he tossed the keys to his partner, "and keep the bumps to a minimum."

"Sure Brick, no problem," Tiffin said as he pushed the gear shift into first and slowly let the clutch out. The Ford gave a slight lurch as he turned down Main toward Highway 31 and Niles.

The Tall Pines was a typical motor court: a free-standing office within a U-shaped court of rooms. Each room had two metal lawn chairs outside the front door. As they entered the office North flashed his badge, "We're looking for a man we believe may be staying here," he began. "Big guy, maybe six one or two, dark hair, that sound familiar?"

The older man looked up from his ledger, "That sounds like Mr. Smith who was staying in number five."

"Was?" Tiffin enquired.

"He checked out about noon yesterday."

"This Smith, he have a first name?" Brick asked.

"John," said the innkeeper adding, "I know it sounds like he made it up, but I don't ask questions. As long as folks keep to themselves and pay their bills, I don't care."

"John Smith, what are the odds of that?" Tiffin said as he made a note in his book.

"When did he check-in?" Brick asked.

"Let me see, I know it was early Sunday morning," he said as he looked at the sign-in register. "Here he is, John Smith arrived Sunday around ten. I told him that check-in wasn't until three, but he paid extra to get into the room early. Said he was tired and needed a nap."

"He say where he was coming from?"

"Nope and I didn't ask."

"You remember anything about his car?"

"Oh yeah, it was a nice one; dark blue Chevy Belair with a white roof. Brand new, too. I commented to the missus that it sure was a beauty."

"Did you notice the license plate number?"

"Not the whole number. The last three numbers were 222, I remember that 'cuz it's my birthday, February 22nd you know, and it was from Illinois. Red with white like ours, but no letters only numbers, and of course it said Land of Lincoln on it."

"You've been helpful. If Mr. Smith does return would you call me please?" North asked as he handed him a business card.

"Oh sure, anything for the police."

As they reached the screen door, Tiffin looked over to North, "Where to next?"

"Let's go see if Doc Howard has gotten anywhere on the autopsy of our blonde."

The County Morgue was on the basement level of Memorial Hospital on the Southside of town. The morning sun reflected off the white outer walls making the building look like it was glowing as they drove into the circular drive. The Morgue itself was covered in ceramic tile from floor to ceiling. A stainless-steel table stood in the center under a large lamp; upon it was the nude body of the blonde they'd seen two days earlier. There were two neat rows of baseball stitches on her chest which formed a 'V' the point of which was at her navel.

"Gentlemen," the doctor said as he looked up for a moment from his work. "How are you feeling Brick?"

"Fine, doc," he lied, "you find anything?"

"More than I thought I would," he said as he pointed toward the body, "your victim was pregnant." Tiffin startled at the news more than did North.

"Anything else?" North said as he wrote in his notebook.

"I'd say she probably died from a heroin overdose, but I won't know until the blood work comes back."

"Why probably?" North queried.

"She's got old needle marks here in the cubital fossa of her arm," he said as he pointed to the crease of the inside of her elbow. "But she's got new marks here in the syndactyly," he added as he walked down and pulled the webbing of her left toes apart. She's got them on her right foot also."

"Why the hell would anyone inject drugs between their toes?" Tiffin asked, "that's gotta hurt like hell."

The doctor walked over to the sink and began washing his hands, "looks like she was trying to hide the fact that she was injecting drugs and the pain isn't a consideration when all one wants to do is get a fix."

"So, the drugs probably killed her, like an overdose?" North asked.

"I'm going to report the cause of death as heart failure secondary to drug overdose."

42

"She had a heart attack?" Tiffin asked incredulously.

"Don't sound shocked, detective," the doctor said, "the body wasn't designed for drugs and something has to give."

"Any way of identifying her?" North asked.

Before the doctor could answer the phone near the door rang. He picked up the receiver, "Doctor Howard," he said. "Where?" he asked as he grabbed a pencil and began writing on a pad on the desk. "Tell them I'll be there in twenty minutes. And tell them I've got North and Tiffin with me."

"What've you got?" North inquired.

"Got us a floater just washed up at Rotary Club Beach."

The detectives got to the scene before the doctor. The midday sun was reflecting off the white sands and North tossed his suitcoat into the Ford and rolled up his sleeves as they walked toward the water where a patrolman was keeping a small crowd of teenagers from getting too close. "Back!" the officer barked toward a teen that had begun to walk behind him.

"No worries Daddy-O, just want to eyeball the dead guy."

"You can eyeball whatever you'd like, from home," North said as he walked up behind the group. "All of you scram before I find a reason to arrest the lot of you."

"Ain't that a bite?" the teen said toward his friends and to North, he added, "no need to bug, Clyde. Come on, this place is Nowheresville."

"What have you got, Phil?" North said toward the officer.

"Got a call about thirty minutes ago. The couple over there found him," he said with a nod toward a park bench, "they called from the Whitcomb hotel."

"Any ID?" Tiffin asked.

"Not that I found, but I gotta admit that I didn't dig around too much."

As they approached the body, they made two observations. The first was that the body was of a middle-aged man of about six feet with blond hair and a scar on his right cheek. The other was that the back of his head was missing.

"I'd think it's safe to say we found our missing doctor," North said toward Tiffin.

"I don't think we'll need Doc Howard to tell us how he died," Tiffin added.

"Not how, but we still don't know why," North said as he reached into the inner jacket pockets of the dead man. "Here we go," he said as he pulled out a large, wet black wallet, "he's got at least two hundred dollars here, so it wasn't robbery. The driver's license is a little soggy but yup," he said as he began reading from it, "Herbert Dalander, 22 Collingwood, Grand Rapids."

The coroner walked up and gave the body a once over.

"Putrefaction has begun," he said mostly to himself, "the heat and the water have exacerbated the process."

"What does that mean, doc?" Tiffin asked.

"It means," North broke in, "that Herbert's guts have started to liquefy."

"And if we move him around too much, we'll probably have him split open," the doctor added.

"God, I hate my job some days," Tiffin said as he turned his back on the corpse.

"You can see that fish have been nibbling at the head wound as well as at his fingers and nose." The doctor added over his shoulder and toward Tiffin.

"I'll read the report," Tiffin replied, obviously uncomfortable with the conversation.

"Weak constitution," North said toward the doctor as he walked back to the Ford. "Let me know what else you come up with." Then to Tiffin, "Let's call Newkirk in Grand Rapids, he's gotta tell Dalander's missus that she's a widow."

North hung up the phone after having shared the news with his counterpart. "I don't envy Newkirk," he said to Tiffin, "I'm thinking Mrs. Dalander is going to take this hard."

"I'd think anyone's wife would take this kind of news hard," Tiffin said as he looked up from the typewriter he was pecking at.

"I think she's going to take it harder than most because the extra money she's been enjoying has just dried up. He also asked me to see if we can get fingerprints from our blonde. There's a club singer who's missing up there that kind of matches our description."

"Why would fingerprints help?" Tiffin asked.

"Because if it's who he thinks it is, she's in the system. That singer has a history of drug arrests."

"Well, now that's progress," Tiffin agreed. "You want to go to the Morgue with me?"

"Nah, you go. I think I'm going to call the Secretary of State's office in Illinois and see if they can give me any information about a white over blue Chevy Belair with a plate that ends in 222."

Tiffin grabbed his hat and jacket while North called the operator to place a call for him. "This is North. I need you to connect me to the Secretary of State's office in Springfield, Illinois."

"Yes, Detective," the operator said, "I'll ring you back when I have them for you."

He thanked the operator, hung up and began to swing his feet onto his desk. His ribs thought better of this and he put his feet down with a heavy thud.

"You got any idea who used you as a punching bag?" Chief Cummings asked as he walked out of his office.

"Some guy by the name of John Smith," North replied.

"Oh good," the Chief said with a sarcastic tone almost as practiced as North's, "at least that narrows it down."

"Don't worry, Chief. I'm going to find him."

"I'm sure you will; do me a favor though," he said looking North directly in the eye, "leave enough of him that we can put him before a jury." He turned back as he was beginning to walk away, "And no falls down the stairs."

"Do my best, boss."

"Do better than that," the chief of police added matter-of-factly before walking away.

A few minutes passed when the old black phone on his desk rang, "North," he answered. "Hold for the Illinois Secretary of State's office. With a few clicks a voice came on, "This is Mrs. McGrath; I understand you're looking for information regarding a car registered in Illinois."

"Yes, I am," North responded. "A '57 Chevrolet Belair, white over blue, with a license plate ending in 222."

"Detective," the state worker said with a sigh, "there are a million possible number combinations and some one thousand license plates ending in those three digits. I don't have the time to go through all those cards to try to find it."

"Do me a favor and take a few minutes and try, will you?" North asked in his most pleasant tone. "It's a new car and probably registered recently. Maybe that'll help."

"I'll give it a half-hour, but no more. I'll call if I find anything."

"I appreciate that," North said sincerely.

North called dispatch to notify them that he was going off-duty for a couple of hours, crushed the Bradmore onto his head and walked back to the Swanson. Inside his room, he gingerly took off his jacket, holster, shirt and pants and eased himself upon the bed. Two nights with almost no sleep had left him absolutely wrung out.

His head had hardly hit the pillow when he fell into a deep sleep. It seemed like only minutes had passed when he was awakened to a pounding at the door. It was only when he opened his eyes and saw how the light had changed in the room that he realized that he had been asleep for some time.

"Hold your horses," he shouted over the pounding. Pushing himself up he grabbed the Colt from its holster and swung the door open with his right hand, the left holding the gun at face-level to Barry Tiffin standing in the hallway.

"Holy crap," Tiffin said as he instinctively moved away from the gun, "put that damn thing away."

"Sorry Tiff," North said as he lowered the weapon, "wasn't expecting you to be the one pounding at my door."

"You checked out of the office four hours ago and I didn't start by pounding. I started by knocking, but you didn't answer. Doesn't matter. Get your pants on, I've got news."

North pulled his wrinkled pants and shirt back on and struggled to bend down to tie his shoes. Tiffin offered no help, knowing that any offer would be refused. "Okay, what's the news?"

"I telexed our dead blonde's fingerprints up to Newkirk."

"And..." North added impatiently.

"And, we've got a name. Michelle Denslow, aged 26. Singer, junky, dead girl. I sent a picture of her up to Newkirk in the afternoon post.

We should hear from him by tomorrow. But he's pretty certain the prints are a match."

"Okay, so we know who she is, how she got here and who brought her. That answers some questions, but raises more."

"Like where'd she die and why they didn't leave her there?" Tiffin added.

"And why did Dalander get killed and why did someone decide they needed me to back away from the case?"

The two of them walked past the storefronts and offices back to the Safety Building. Tiffin headed back upstairs, North stopped in to check on Sylvia. She and a half dozen other women had their back to the door, all of them seated in tall swivel chairs facing the switchboard. Their hands moved quickly as they connected calls. North noticed that it didn't seem that any of them had to look at their boards; their fingers just knew where to place the plugs as they said, "Pease hold."

"Hey Syl," North said quietly as he walked up to her.

"Brick!" she said in a voice that was much louder than the ones around her. Then in a lower voice added, "Oh my God, I heard you got into a fight, but you look awful. Are you okay?"

"It looks worse than it is doll," he said with a fake smile. "Don't worry about me, you know I can take care of myself."

Sylvia looked toward her supervisor, "Midge, you mind if I take five?"

A matronly looking woman turned and looked at her and North. "Go ahead, Sylvia, just don't take too long, a couple of the girls are getting ready to end their shifts."

"Right back," she said as she and North exited into the hallway.

"I want you to spend the night," North said frankly as soon as they were alone.

"Brick, you don't look like you need company tonight."

"I don't want you to be alone. I'll tell you why later. What time do you get off shift?"

"Eight o'clock," Sylvia said, sounding concerned. "What's going on?"

"I'll be waiting for you."

"I need to go by my place and get a few things," she said.

"I'll go with you. We can stay at your place if you want."

"You're making me nervous."

"It'll be okay. I'll be here at eight."

North kissed her on the forehead and took the elevator to the second floor. He found a note on his desk. "Illinois called back. They have two possible matches for you," Tiffin said as North read the card.

"I see there's a guy from Carbondale, that's near St. Louis I think, and one from Skokie which is Chicagoland."

"The Skokie one looked interesting to me. See the name the car is registered to?"

"Alberto Como," North said with some interest. "Lucky Como. How the hell is he connected to all this?"

"I don't know," Tiffin answered, "but it's gotta be something for a bigtime mobster like Lucky Como to have an interest in it."

"You know what I like about bigtime guys Tiff?"

"What's that?"

"When they fall, it's so much more satisfying than when the little guys do."

# Chapter 4

"I wish you would tell me what's going on," Sylvia whispered to North as they walked towards her Nash in the city parking lot.

"Let's get to the car first," North said as he took her by the elbow and hurried her along.

Once in the car, she turned onto Main and towards her studio in the old Sheffield building just east of downtown.

"The guy who roughed me up last night is on the payroll of one of Chicago's biggest mobsters. He threatened me, and you," he said as he looked her direction, "if I continued to look into this case."

They drove in silence for most of the three-minute trip to her apartment building. "Don't you think you're being a little overly protective?" She said as she turned into the drive.

"I don't think that these goons would have any problem hurting you if they thought it would get me off their case."

"I'm a big girl," she argued.

"And I'm a big guy and that didn't stop them."

Sylvia's apartment was in stark contrast to the room at the Swanson where North lived. Whereas the only thing in his room that identified it as his were his clothes, Sylvia's studio was filled with mementos and feminine touches. She switched on a table lamp, the shade of which was covered with a rose-colored silk scarf that cast a warm glow around the small room. "If you're going to stay here, I guess you should make yourself at home," she said as she stepped into the small bathroom.

North took off his jacket and the leather shoulder holster and put them both on the overstuffed chair in the corner. He took the .38 from the holster, opened the cylinder and gave it a spin before clicking it shut. He put the gun on the coffee table and sat down on the sofa which gave him a view of both the door to the hall and the window which overlooked the street.

A few minutes later she walked out of the bathroom. Gone was the severe skirt, stiffly starched white blouse and heels, replaced by a short kimono-style robe that revealed her thighs. "I don't have much to eat around here," she remarked as she stepped toward the small counter which housed a refrigerator, sink and two-burner stove. Opening the fridge, she bent down to look in while North took a moment to look at her. "I've got some ham and cheese and can make us a sandwich if you'd like."

"Sure doll, I'm not that hungry."

"What have you eaten today?" she asked with a motherly sound to her voice.

"Today?"

"Yeah, today," she insisted.

"Hmmm. Nothing I guess."

"Then ham and cheese it is."

A few minutes later she brought out two small plates each with a sandwich, two glasses and a bottle of beer. "I've only got the one," she said with a nod to the brown bottle, "so we'll have to split it."

North's jaw ached as he chewed the sandwich. Sylvia tuned the radio to WCFL out of Chicago. "They won't play Elvis."

"What's that doll?" North said as he finished his share of the beer.

"This station has banned Elvis' records. Crazy, huh?" she said as Pat Boone sang 'April Love.'

"I guess," North muttered trying to remember who Elvis was. "What shift you working tomorrow?"

"Same as today," she said, "ten until eight."

"Okay, we'll figure out the morning when we get there." Once they had both finished eating, she cleared the dishes and put them into the small sink.

"You tired, Brick?"

"I had a nap this afternoon, so I'm not too bad, but yeah, I'm tired."

"Why don't I make up the bed and we can stretch out?" she offered as she gently shooed North from the sofa. With his help, she slid the coffee table under the window and removed the seat cushions revealing a convertible double-bed. She pulled on the strap and the bed folded out. She brought two pillows from the closet and placed them at the head of the bed, "Voila!" she said as she turned off the light and stepped out of the robe. By the light of the radio dial North could make out her soft curves under the chiffon boxers and sleeveless top she was wearing.

North kicked off his shoes, pulled off his shirt, pants and socks and stretched out on the bed. Sylvia began to cuddle up next to him but then pulled back, "Oh, I'm sorry, did I hurt you?"

"Doc Howard's got my ribs bound up so tight that an atom bomb couldn't shake 'em," he said adding, "I'll let you know if you press too hard."

She gently poured herself into his right side, "what's going on that they want to hurt you?"

"They want me to stop investigating the murder of one Michelle Denslow and Doctor Dalander."

"Is that the girl's name?" Sylvia asked.

"Yeah, a lounge singer I understand."

"Were she and Dalander a thing?"

"I'm thinking maybe they were. She was carrying somebody's baby."

"Oh my God, how awful!" Sylvia cried, "But why do you think they were killed?"

"We know she was a junky and that Dalander was making a lot of trips to Chicago and then traveling around the state here. So, if I had to make a guess, I'd say that he was probably moving heroin for someone in Chicago and maybe got behind on his payments."

"Who's this mobster you were talking about?"

"Como."

"Como? Like Perry Como?" she asked.

North's smile hurt, "I don't think they're related."

"So maybe Dalander owed this Como guy money and he bumps off the doc and his girl?"

"That's what I gotta figure out."

It wasn't long before Sylvia stopped asking questions and North realized that she had fallen asleep. The convertible was terribly uncomfortable on his ribs, as was Sylvia leaning into them, so he gently removed himself and sat propped up in the overstuffed chair. He too finally drifted off to sleep after having listened to the Top-40 at least twice.

Sylvia found North asleep in the big chair when she got up in the morning. He'd stacked the two sofa cushions and was using them as an ottoman for his feet. She softly brushed against him as she leaned in and kissed him on the head. North stirred and she noticed the gun in his hand. "Don't mind me, Brick," she whispered. She grabbed a couple of things from the closet and, stepping out of her nightclothes, pulled on a pair of capris and a sweater, and slipped her feet into a pair of worn flats. She got the percolator going and picking up her purse, quietly made her way toward the door and the Dubois bakery for something for breakfast for the two of them.

The smell of coffee woke North. With a yawn and cautious stretch, he looked around the room. "Syl?" he asked. He got up and looked into the bathroom. The only other space was the closet and it was too small to step into. He noticed her nightclothes on the foot of the bed and the fact her purse was gone.

"Dammit all to hell!" he said under his breath as he quickly pulled his clothes on. He slipped the gun under his arm and was out the door. He noticed that her car was not in the parking lot and walked to the police callbox on the corner. As soon as the operator answered he said, "This is Detective North, put me up to the squad room." "Yes, detective," the female voice replied.

"Tiffin," Barry answered.

"Tiff, I spent the night at Sylvia's and she and her car are gone."

"Maybe you should take the hint," Tiffin kidded.

"I'm serious, Tiff. I told her that she was in danger and when I woke this morning she was gone."

"Where are you?" Tiffin asked.

"Outside the Sheffield at Main and Second."

"I'll be there in ten," Tiffin replied before the line disconnected.

North lit a cigarette and looked around. A streetcar passed heading toward downtown with a dozen or so passengers. The milkman was making his way back to Consumer's Dairy having completed his morning rounds and he could hear the playful sound of kids as they walked to school. By the time the Pall Mall was burned to his fingers, the Ford Mainline had stopped to pick him up. He climbed into the passenger seat and slammed the door. "Head toward downtown, let's see if we can spot her car."

"What's she drive?" Tiffin asked.

"Red '54 Rambler," North said as the Ford pulled away from the curb. They took Main almost down to the Safety Building when North shouted, "Stop! Back up!" Tiffin stopped and did as directed. There in the alley between the Farmer & Merchant's Bank and Aristo's cleaners was the Nash, its driver's door ajar.

"Shit," North said as he jumped from the still rolling car. He got to the Nash in just a couple of strides and looked inside. Sylvia's purse was there, but she was not. "God-dammit!" he shouted in a loud enough voice that a couple of passersby's stopped and looked at him. Tiffin showed them his badge and asked them to keep moving.

North pounded his fist on the hood of the Nash, "why the hell didn't she listen to me?"

"She probably thought you were exaggerating," Tiffin said as he approached with a black case from the trunk of the Ford, "Let's see if we can lift any prints off this before we get it taken to the city yard."

Tiffin carefully opened the jar of lampblack and with a soft brush swirled the fine dust around the door pillar, handle and inside the upper edge of the window frame. "We've got a bunch of prints here," he said as he applied cellophane tape onto the most distinct prints which he then pulled off and stuck onto cards. "Got a couple of good-sized prints here, too big to be Sylvia's," he said toward North. "You use this door, or drive the car?"

"No," North said in a frustrated tone, "I haven't driven her car if that's what you're asking.

"Then I can be sure these prints aren't yours."

From a callbox down the street, Tiffin asked for a wrecker to come to pick up the Nash. It wasn't long before it was there and the car was being towed away. North tossed Sylvia's purse onto the bench seat between him and his partner as Tiffin turned the car back into traffic and toward the Safety Building. The Building was buzzing when they walked in. "Is it true?" Midge, the switchboard manager, asked as they walked toward the elevator.

"I'm afraid so," Tiffin offered as he passed.

"I can't believe it," she said, "why would someone take Sylvia?"

"I don't know, but we're going to find out and find her," Tiffin shouted down the corridor from the elevator which North was holding open for him.

In the squad room, North took a look at the fingerprint cards that Tiffin had placed on the desk. "Where we going to start, Brick? Tiffin asked.

"I'm thinking the Chicago PD and the FBI would probably be the best places." They prepared the necessary paperwork and Telexed the fingerprints to the FBI in Detroit and the Chicago police department. "You can sit around here and wait if you want," North said once the machine had finished sending the information, "but I'm going to see if anyone saw anything this morning."

He pushed his hat onto his head, crushed the cigarette he'd been smoking and walked to the elevator. He looked at it for a second before turning and heading toward the stairwell.

On the street, he walked to the dry cleaners next to where the Nash had been found. The smell of the cleaning solvent filled the air. An older woman looked up from the Mangle she was using to press what appeared to be a tablecloth. "May I help you?" she asked as she wiped her brow with the back of her hand.

"There was a red car that was abandoned in the alley this morning," North said as he showed her his badge, "I'm wondering if you saw anything unusual."

"I saw the car being towed about thirty minutes ago," she offered.

"Nothing earlier?"

"I got down just as it was being towed, but my husband may have seen something, he came down about six-thirty."

"Is he here, may I speak to him?"

"Charlie!" she shouted over the sound of the cleaning equipment.

"What?!" he said as he walked up from the back of the shop.

"This policeman wants to ask about the car in the alley this morning."

"Your wife says that you were down here maybe ninety minutes before we found the Nash next to your shop this morning. Did you see or hear anything?"

"Hear anything?! Can't hear anything over this," he said as he swept his hand toward the equipment.

"See anything unusual this morning?" North asked trying to hold his impatience at bay.

"Well, now that you mention it, there was a blue car that sat across the street for the longest time this morning."

"What the car look like?"

"Oh, I think it was a Chevy, two-tone."

"White over dark blue?"

"Yeah, that was it."

"Get a look at the driver?"

"Not real good," he said as he pushed his glasses back up his nose, "dark suit and hat is about the only thing I could see."

"Was there anyone with him?"

"Yeah, there was a kid with him."

"A kid?" North repeated.

"Some punk-looking kid. White t-shirt, no hat. Had his hair slicked back."

"How old would you say the kid was?"

"I don't know. Old enough he should be working somewhere. I'd say maybe eighteen or so."

"You've been helpful," North said as he handed over a business card, "call me if you think of anything else."

"Is someone in trouble?" the shopkeeper asked.

"Oh, someone has definitely found trouble," North said as he pushed the screen door open.

He walked across the street to where the Chevy had been parked. There were a number of filtered cigarette butts where the passenger door would have been. In the street, there were also a half-dozen butts, these without filters. "Someone was waiting a while," he thought to himself. He peered into the windows of the lady's hat shop in front of which the car had been. It was still closed. He looked at his watch, it was a quarter of ten, fifteen minutes before the shop would open.

He checked with the shoe repair shop next door and learned that the owner had seen the car parked out front. "Thought it was weird," the owner said.

"How so?" North inquired.

"Well, they just sat there like they was waiting for someone, you know, the guy behind the wheel kept looking at his watch."

"What can you tell me about the two in the car?"

"Kind of looked like a father and son the way there were carrying on."

"What do you mean?"

"I couldn't hear, but it looked like the driver was, you know, telling the younger guy off."

"What else did you see?"

"I was busy resoling a pair of shoes, so it wasn't like I was watching them all the time."

"I understand," North said, "but anything you did see might be helpful."

"The kid did get out of the car and run across the street at one point. Almost got hit by a car. Woman had to slam on her brakes to keep from hitting him."

"What kind of car was it?"

"Small red car, maybe a Rambler."

"What happened next?"

"Driver got out and I saw him talking to the woman in the red car. Figured he was apologizing for his kid."

"Anything else?"

"Sorry, looked back down at my work and when I looked up, they were leaving."

"What do you mean, leaving?"

"The red car was gone and the blue Chevy was driving away. But you know what? The kid was in the backseat when they left. That was odd, wasn't it? You know what else was odd?" he asked, "the kid had a patch of white hair on the right side of his head, over the ear. All black but that one patch."

"You've been very helpful," North said as he walked toward the door.

"Tiff," he shouted as soon as he'd turned into the squad room, "It was Como's goon and he had some punk ass kid helping him."

"I'm not surprised by the goon. But where'd the kid come in?"

"Grab your hat; let's find out."

There were only a couple of places in LaSalle Harbor where dropouts and beatniks hung out, both in the older part of the city down near the harbor. The detectives checked out the first joint, an old bar that had been shut down numerous times for violating the Sunday laws. They left with no answers.

The second joint was a pool hall that offered greasy food and bottled beer. The proprietor was busy grilling some hamburgers for a group of teens sitting in a corner booth. "Shouldn't you kids be in school?" Tiffin asked as they walked in. "Shouldn't you be in school?" one of the kids mocked as his friends laughed.

North walked up to the counter, "I'm looking for a kid who might hang out here. Has a patch of white hair over one ear."

"You're talking about the Billy Bryant," the man said as he wiped his hands on the apron that was tied about his waist. "Just missed the little asshole too," he added.

"He was here this morning?" North asked sternly.

"Came in about an hour ago like some bigshot; wanted to pay for a ten-cent Coke with a twenty-dollar bill."

"That so?" Tiffin asked.

"Yup. Like I keep that kind of money around here. Especially first thing in the morning. Idiot punk."

"This Bryant, he live around here?" North asked.

"He squats around here wherever he can. Don't exactly know where. Maybe you should ask some of his friends," he said as he nodded toward the teens in the corner.

North and Tiffin walked toward the booth. "Where can we find Billy Bryant?" North asked as he hovered over the table. "I don't know," one of the kids said, "maybe with your mother?" His friends had just started to laugh when North grabbed the teen by the throat and lifted him out of the booth. North slammed him into the wall hard enough to knock a sign down. Tiffin stood at the booth making certain none of the other three teens stood up.

"I don't have time for your smart-ass comments," North said as he stared into the kid's eyes, "Where's Bryant?"

"He usually flops down on Smith Court, the empty boarding house," the teen answered.

"See, that wasn't so hard," North said as he released his grip. As soon as he was freed, the kid took a swing at North which the detective could have avoided but the tape ribs prevented him from swerving. The punch landed solidly against the back of his head, knocking the Bradmore across the room. North turned and with a left-cross laid the kid out. "Which of you tough guys are next?" he said as he turned back to the table.

The remaining boys looked at him in shock. "Get your friend and get the hell out of here." North said. The three helped the loudmouth up and left in a hurry. North tossed a dollar on the counter, "for the burgers they ordered," he said as he and Tiffin walked outside. The four teens were already a half block away by the time they got outside.

"Let's see if Mr. Bryant is home," he said as he brushed the dust off his hat and they climbed into the car.

Smith Court was only a couple of blocks away. It was in the original part of the city, the houses there dating back to the 1860s. The boarding house wasn't too hard to find on a street that was only one block long. "Fitting isn't it?" Tiffin asked as he pulled in front.

"How's that?"

"The boarding house is boarded up."

"Let's figure out how young Mr. Bryant gets in." He walked around the west side of the building, Tiffin the east; they met on the north. It was there that they saw between the boards that the backdoor was ajar. With a little effort, they swung a couple of boards out of their way and entered what had been the kitchen.

"Smells like shit in here," Tiffin said as they walked in.

North took in the odor which assaulted his nostrils, "There probably is shit in here,"

The house was dark save for the light that crept in between the boards over the windows. As they looked around the first-floor rooms, they found all of them empty, but it was obvious that the house was being used by squatters.

They made their way up the creaking stairs to the second floor. On the floor of third room they looked into, they found Bryant passed out on a dirty mattress. A needle lay next to him. "Is he breathing?" Tiffin asked as North neared him.

"Lucky for him, he is. He's just passed out."

66

They managed to drag his limp form down the stairs and to the car. Bryant found himself handcuffed to a table in the interrogation room when we came out of his drug-induced nap.

"Good morning, sunshine," North said as Bryant tried to focus his eyes on his surroundings.

"Where am I?"

"You've got to be joking right? Hey, Tiff, Bryant here wants to know where he is," North said to his partner.

"Oh, here?" Tiffin said looking toward Bryant, "this is Disneyland," he said referring to the park that had opened in California.

"Look at me, Bryant," North said in a voice that was loud enough to startle the youth. "At the moment, I'm arresting you for violation of the Harrison Narcotics Act for possession of heroin," he leaned forward until his face was just inches from Bryant, "and I'm going to add to that kidnapping, and perhaps two murders for dessert."

"Murder!" Bryant said as he tried to push back from the desk, the handcuffs holding it and him firmly together. "I ain't murdered no one."

"You know what's funny? I've never arrested anyone who's admitted to murder." North grabbed a chair, spun it around and sat over it with his arms resting on the back. "Why don't we talk about the kidnapping then?"

"I don't know nothing about no kidnapping."

"Why don't I believe you?" then to his partner, "You believe him, Tiff?"

"Nah, Brick, I don't believe a word he's said."

North stood up and walked around behind Bryant, "It would be good if you would reconsider your answer," he said as he placed his large fist into Bryant's side knocking him sideways and the air out of him. "You want to maybe change that answer?" North said as he circled back in front of him.

"It wasn't no kidnapping," the youth said.

"What do you mean it wasn't kidnapping?" North asked with venom in his voice.

"Well, she wasn't no kid. And I was told that she was just a whore, so what's it matter?"

North backhanded Bryant with such force that the chair went out from under him and he was left hanging from the table by the handcuffs. Tiffin helped him back up and pushed the chair under him.

"The woman you helped take works for the police department and she's a personal friend of mine," North snapped. "Maybe you ought to tell me everything you know. Let's start with who the man was that you were with."

"I don't know who he is."

"You kidnapped a woman together, what do you mean you don't know who he is?"

"He was outside the pool hall down in the Flats last night looking for someone to help him with a little job. He offered me twenty dollars to help him this morning."

"So, someone you don't know offers you twenty dollars and you don't think there's anything hinky about it?"

"Two day's pay for a couple hours work? I don't ask questions."

"Where'd you take the girl?" Tiffin asked as North lit a cigarette.

"I don't know where it was."

"What do you mean?" North said as he blew smoke out his nose.

"I was in the back of the car holding her down and wasn't watching where we were going."

"Was she alive?" Tiffin asked.

"Yeah, she was alive alright," Bryant offered. "We tied her up and left her in this cottage near a little lake."

"What did the cottage look like?" North asked leaning in again.

"I don't know; old?"

North took a drag on the cigarette, as Tiffin said, "Dirt road or paved? What color was the cottage? Are there other cottages around it?"

Bryant looked between the two detectives. "Dirt for a ways off the main road. The cottage was white, but all faded like, and yeah, there were a bunch of other cottages around."

North stood up and walked behind Bryant again, "I'm really getting tired of this conversation. What direction did your friend drive when you left town?"

"East, I guess. Inland, you know?"

"Tiff, take him down to holding before I actually do lose my temper," and then to Bryant, "You better hope I find my friend alive you little sonofabitch or I'll come down on you so hard your grandchildren will feel it."

Bryant looked away from North's anger as Tiffin undid the cuffs holding him to the table and latched them behind his back. Tiffin pushed Bryant out of the room and past a gauntlet of police officers, all of whom wanted at least one minute alone with him.

"Is this the punk who took Sylvia?" One of the older officers asked.

"It is," Tiffin offered as they walked toward the elevator that would lead to the holding cells in the basement.

"Oh, good," the officer said. "Guess what kid? I'm gonna be your nursemaid tonight. I'll see that you're all nice and tucked in." There was laughter among the officers as Chief Cummings stepped out of his office.

"Detective Tiffin," he shouted over the laughter.

"Yes, chief?"

"Not that I would mind, but make sure he doesn't fall down the steps."

"We're going to take the elevator," Tiffin said over his shoulder.

"Too bad," one of the officers said as they went back to their duties.

# Chapter 5

Tiffin watched the doctor finish sewing up Dalander's body "You know, in a few short years we've gone from delinquents and negro kids using heroin, to well-to-do kids from good families who are using it after having used marijuana for a while." The detective found himself uniquely mesmerized watching Howard tie neat baseball stitches into the chest of the corpse.

"I don't get it, why would good kids start injecting this poison into themselves?"

"The feds increased the penalty for marijuana use, so supply dropped and prices went up. At the same time, the price of heroin has remained cheap."

Howard looked up from his work, "And heroin is much more addictive than marijuana."

"Yep, that about sums it up. They get some and they want more. So, what are you listing as the cause of death for Dalander?"

Howard washed his hands and pointed his thumb toward the body, "My colleague here died of a gunshot wound to the back of his head." The coroner put a finger to the back of Tiffin's head. "The bullet entered the back of his skull to the left of the midline and just above the large venous channel, which it severed. It penetrated the dura mater, passed through the left posterior lobe of the brain into the left lateral ventricle, and came to rest just above the anterior portion of the left corpus striatum. It fractured both orbital plates of the frontal bone which pushed fragments of bone into the brain."

"So, he died pretty much instantly," the detective said as he fought back the wave of nausea that swept over him.

"No, not that he would have survived this grievous of a wound, but he was still alive when he went into the water," he said as he dried his hands. "But I am listing the cause of death as the gunshot wound to the head."

"Do you know how long he's been dead?

"Hard to be exact because of his time in the water, but I figure two or three days."

Tiffin made a note in his book, "So he might have died Sunday night or Monday morning?"

Doc Howard gave a slight shrug, "That's a reasonable assumption."

"Did you recover the bullet?"

"It's there on the table, looks like a 9mm to me; longer than a .38 bullet, but about the same diameter, maybe from a German Luger."

"Odd choice of weapon."

"To each his own, detective. To each his own."

Back at the squad room, Tiffin caught North up on the autopsy results. North paid little interest in the report. "Sonofabitch," North snorted as he scanned a map of Douglas County. "I marked out the radius of where they could have taken Sylvia in a thirty-minute drive. There are forty-three lakes in the county and thirty-one of them are in that radius."

"Where should we start looking?"

"I think we start with those closest to the Harbor and work our way out."

"We'll find her Brick"

"And we'll find him," North said referring to the big man, "and I will make him pay."

"You're not going North. I need you and Tiffin to concentrate on finding out more about Denslow and Dalander." Chief Cummings spoke as he walked across the squad room. "I've assigned three patrolmen to begin a search of the cottages in Douglas County."

North began to argue with the Chief, but Tiffin stepped between them, "Come on Brick, let's go," and with a hand on his partner's shoulder, turned him toward and out the door of the squad room.

Once behind the wheel of the Ford, North turned to his partner, "Okay, we know that Como's goon is still in the area and that Chevy he's driving stands out and it needs gas."

"So where do we start?"

"Let's start at the gas stations."

It took the better part of two hours to visit each of the fourteen stations in the city, and at each they met the same shake of the head. Tiffin threw his hat onto the car's seat as he climbed in and wiped his brow with his handkerchief, "where do we go now?"

"Smith spent some time in Niles, and I doubt if he'd trust his luck hanging around those parts. Let's head down the coast a few miles and see if we find anything." North turned the car onto M-11 and drove south toward the Grand Mere area along the coast. About five miles outside of town they stopped into a Sinclair station. The bell chimed twice as they drove over the pneumatic cord. A teenager in a white uniform ran toward the car.

"Fill 'er up?"

North stepped from the Ford and made sure the kid could see his badge, "looking for some information."

"Gosh, sure, what kind of information?"

"Looking for a guy, drives a brand-new Chevy Belair, white over dark blue. Illinois plates."

The kid perked up, "yeah, with a Turbo-Fire V-8 under the hood. That car'll agitate the gravel all right."

Tiffin grabbed his notepad, "So, you've seen it?"

"Yeah, it's been in a couple of times."

North put his full attention to the youth, "when's the last time you saw it?"

"Don't know exactly, maybe about lunchtime."

"What direction did it go when it left?"

"South toward the Mere," the teen said as he pointed with his forehead.

Grand Mere State Park was a large area of primordial forest, bogs and sand dunes. There were at least a hundred homes along miles of dirt roads.

"If he's holding out in the Mere it'll take days to track him down."

"Gotta think smart, Tiff," North said as he turned back toward the city.

"Wait, aren't we going to start looking for Smith?"

"Of course we are, partner. But, let's try to be smart about this."

Ten minutes later they were pulling into the county courthouses' parking lot. Tiffin looked confused, "What are we doing here?"

North pulled on his jacket and crushed the fedora onto his head, "the Register of Deeds office."

"Ah!" his partner responded as they walked up the steps of the old sandstone building.

Tiffin dropped a dime into the payphone in the lobby and dialed the number for the station, as the phone rang the dime dropped back into the coin slot. He was just putting it back into his pocket when an operator picked up, "LaSalle Harbor police."

"This is detective Tiffin, get me the chief's office."

While he caught the chief up, North was busy with the clerk at the Register's counter, "I don't care if it takes you all day, I need you to look at property which is registered to Alberto Como in the county."

"There are twenty-three towns and cities, dozens of villages and unincorporated areas. What you're asking is going to take us days to look into."

"Let's narrow it down, doll," North flirted as he leaned on the counter, even though his ribs were aching. "Why don't we look at Lincoln and maybe Lake Township. How long will that take."

The clerk, a twenty-something blonde, blushed, "not as much area to look at. I'll pull the plat maps." Each township was thirty-six square miles and each had a few large leather-bound books of maps. The books were placed upon a wooden table behind the counter and the two detectives and the clerk each took one. They were each on their second book when Tiffin looked toward North, "What kind of name is 'Esportazioni Italiane?'"

"Italian Exports."

"What's that?"

"It translates Italian exports. I think you found our property. What book is that in?"

"Lincoln Township Book Three, it includes the south end of Grand Mere."

"Then that's where we're going."

North made some notes and thanked the clerk. She smiled broadly, "Come back again."

Back in the parking lot, Tiffin asked for the car keys, "Why don't you let me drive?"

"What's up, Tiff?"

"It's mid-afternoon and we haven't had lunch. I want to grab a sandwich and get our heads on straight before we go find Smith."

"Lunch can wait!" North shot back, "Sylvia can't."

"And if we're not on our best we aren't worth shit. Fifteen minutes and we're heading for the Mere."

"Okay, you're probably right. Last thing I had to eat was a ham and cheese that Syl gave me last night. But I'm driving."

North parked at the curb in front of the Fifth Wheel and waited while Tiffin ran in and grabbed a couple of sandwiches. Back in the car, Tiffin unwrapped his roast beef, crumpled the waxed paper it had been wrapped in and threw it out the window. North's sandwich was on the dash, sliding back and forth as he drove.

About ten miles south of town they pulled off M-11 and onto a dirt lane that wound them three-quarters of a mile around the stands of trees, dunes and ponds that led toward Lake Michigan. North pulled the car off the road and parked behind a stand of birch trees. He took the black notepad from his pocket and looked at the notes he'd made, "We shouldn't be too far from the property, why don't we take a hike?"

They exited the Ford and walked cautiously up the dirt lane that had grass growing up the middle. Around a bend and half-hidden behind a stand of trees stood a two-story house which, while made of fieldstone, had a classic elegance. North pointed toward the blue Chevy parked on the side of the house and, looking at Tiffin, put a finger to his lips. He made a sign for his partner to go around the other side of the house and that he would check out the car.

Tiffin made his way toward the house trying to use the trees and shrubs as cover. North bent low and ran toward the Chevy. The windows were down and he made a quick look around. On the floorboard of the back was a lady's slip-on shoe. He fought the urge to take the shoe and crouching, moved back to where he left Tiffin.

Just as he got to the point where he could see the front of the house, he was met by Smith who had Tiffin in a chokehold and a Luger to the detective's head, "You know something North, you got balls. I beat the shit out of you, I take your whore and you're still dogging me." Tiffin pulled at the big man's arm which held him tight. "You know what else Detective? You're stupid trying to track me down."

"But I did," North shouted back as he pulled the Colt from under his right arm and aimed toward Smith's head, "Now, let go of my partner and we all walk away from here."

"That ain't going to happen. Get away from the car," Smith used Tiffin as a shield and moved toward the Chevy.

"Drop your gun and release him."

"I don't think you understand that you're not in control here, Pal."

"And you don't understand that you're not leaving here."

Smith jabbed the gun into Tiffin's temple and tightened his grip until the detective's lips were blue, "Oh, I'm leaving here alright and your partner is here to make sure nothing happens to me." He began dragging the detective toward the car again.

Tiffin looked at North, blinked his eyes tightly for a second and gave a nod. In that moment he lifted his feet from under himself, leaned forward, and allowed his weight to pull on Smith's arm. Smith took his attention away from North for a heartbeat. At that moment a red dot appeared in the middle of the big man's forehead. The sound of the .38 reverberated off the stone on the front of house. The big man fell one way, Tiffin the other. "You okay, Tiff?"

Rubbing his throat, he stood up and looked down at Smith's body. "Holy shit, Brick. He's the only one who knew where Sylvia is."

"We found him, we'll find Sylvia. But I'm not going to tell Kaye and your kids that your body is with Doc Howard. Now, let's see what we can find around here."

They walked away from Smith's lifeless body and to the house. With gun in hand, each quietly made their way through the front door. Tiffin took the rooms to the left, North to the right. After having made sure the house was empty, they used the phone in the kitchen to call Cummings.

Within twenty minutes not only was the Chief there, but also the County Sheriff, as the house was outside their jurisdiction. Doc Howard pulled in just behind the Sheriff.

"Your man a little trigger happy, Pete?" the Sheriff said as he walked up to where Cummings and Tiffin were talking. "Nice shot," he remarked as he stepped over Smith's body.

"Not much in the house Chief," Tiffin said as he led Cummings and the Sheriff, Red Wilson, through the front door. Inside they saw what Tiffin meant. Most of the furniture was covered with drop cloths except for the kitchen table and a bed on the second floor. A brown leather Mark Cross suitcase sat open on the foot of the bed.

"Where's North?" Cummings asked as he looked through the case.

"He was going to look through the car and see if he can come up with anything."

Cummings looked at the expensive leather suitcase, "Well, there's not much here," and with that, he turned the case over and with a pencil moved the dirty shirts and underwear around. A quick look in the bathroom revealed nothing out of the ordinary; a leather shaving kit that matched the suitcase was open on the vanity. Tiffin turned the kit out and found a small pouch the same color as the lining on the bottom. He unzipped it and found a small vial of white powder and a hypodermic syringe. He also found a stack of some fifty twenty-dollar bills.

"Looks like he was a hophead too," Tiffin said as he put the items back into the pouch.

The Sheriff, whose keen eye was on the cash said, "Since this is my jurisdiction, I think I better take that into evidence."

"Like hell, Red," Cummings argued. "My detectives, my missing employee, two murders in my beat, I think this is better kept in my evidence room than yours.

"You accusing me of malfeasance?"

"Nope, I just know I can trust my men to be able to find this when we need it for evidence, that's all."

The three of them walked out a side door as North was leaning against the Belair, a Pall Mall stuck to his lip. "Was wondering when you would get here. I think you might be interested in a couple of things I found."

North grabbed a large brick-shaped package wrapped in brown paper and tied with string. "What say we look at what we've got?" With his pocket knife he cut a small slit into the paper and dug his knife in. On the blade was a white substance. "Wow!" Tiffin exclaimed.

"Yup, maybe a pound of smack, but that's not all." He held up a datebook, "There's a couple of interesting things in Mr. Smith's diary, or De Luca actually. Here's his license, Christopher De Luca, from Skokie. But look at Sunday's page."

The three others leaned in. "Meet HD 11 PM Lakeland." the sheriff read aloud, "HD?"

North filled in the blanks, "Gotta be Herbert Dalander, our dead doctor from Grand Rapids."

"Okay, so why would a mobster who has a pound of heroin in the trunk of this car and enough for a down payment on a house be meeting our doctor at an out-of-the-way airport?" Tiffin thought aloud.

"Why indeed," Chief Cummings added, "why indeed."

Tiffin drove the Ford and North followed him back to the Safety Building in the Belair. Once inside they cataloged the contents of the car, suitcase and shaving kit and, along with the cash, logged everything into evidence.

It was almost twilight when they returned from the evidence locker. "I'm going home and tuck my kids into bed. You heading home?" Tiffin asked as he grabbed his coat.

"No, I think I'll have another go at young Mister Bryant, see if he remembers any more than he did. Maybe twenty-four hours in lockup have softened him a bit."

"You want me to stick around?"

"Nah, go give your wife a squeeze. I got this." North and Tiffin walked down to the first floor together; Tiffin headed for the doors, North continued down to the basement level where the holding cells were. The basement smelled of mold, damp paper, and as he got nearer the cells, human sweat.

"Hey Lou," North said toward an older officer seated at a wooden desk outside the barred door that led into the corridor where the cells were. "How many in there tonight?"

The grey-haired officer looked up from the newspaper crossword he was working on, "Just the kid you brought in."

"Don't you have to take a shit or something?" North asked as he looked first to the cells, then to the officer.

"Oh, yeah," He offered, giving the detective a knowing nod, "I sure need to see a man about a horse. I'll just leave my keys on the desk for safekeeping," he added as he walked toward the stairs.

North waited until Lou was up to the landing and out of sight before he rolled the newspaper tightly, twisting it into a stick, grabbed the keys, unlocked the outer door and walked into the dimly lit corridor.

82

There were four holding cells, two on either side of the aisle; each had three walls of concrete blocks and one of bars from floor to ceiling. In each was a metal cot, a thin mattress with a thinner blanket, a toilet and a sink. Bryant was in the far cell lying on the bunk with his back to the world.

"Hey Billy," North said as he slid the heavy key into the lock on the cell, "why don't you and I have a little talk."

"I ain't got nothin' to say to you."

"Oh, I think you've probably got a lot to say. Get on your feet."

"I ain't got to do nothin'."

North drove the end of the rolled-up newspaper into Bryant's back with force. The youth jumped up. "That fuckin' hurt."

North pulled the kid off the bunk, "That was the idea, Billy. Why don't you try to remember where you took the woman."

"I told you that I don't know. Why don't you find the guy who drove and ask him?"

"Oh, I found him and he's not talking."

"I'm not talkin' either."

"He's not talking because I put a bullet between his eyes."

North's words startled Bryant who stepped back until his calves were against the cot.

"You can't shoot me! I'm in jail and people will hear you!"

North swung the roll of newspaper which crashed against the side of the kid's head, striking him firmly on the ear. Bryant stumbled and fell onto the cot.

"Get your ass on your feet, punk," North commanded. When Bryant refused, the detective pulled him up by his shirt. "You're going to tell me where you took the woman."

"I don't know where we took her!" Bryant said through tears.

North pulled the newspaper up over his head and Bryant put his hands up to block the blow. Instead of the head, North swung the paper in a hard thrust downward which scraped against youth's crotch. With a grunt, Bryant instinctively pulled his hands away from his face and covered his groin. North quickly swung the paper against Bryant's head and the youth crumpled onto the floor, tears rolling down his face.

"You want to a big man, so listen up. What I've just given you is nothing compared to what you're going to get in the state pen. The men over in Jackson," North said referring to the State Penitentiary, "have a way of chewing little boys like you up."

North softened his tone, "Now, why don't you tell me where you took the woman."

"I don't know," the words came out in sobs, "I was stoned, I was in the backseat, I wasn't paying no attention."

"Bullshit!"

"I'm tellin' you the truth!"

"You wouldn't know the truth if it bit you in the ass!"

"I swear, I don't know! I don't know!"

"If I find out you're holding anything back from me I will make you wish I had put a bullet between your eyes!"

North walked out of the cell and slammed the door behind him. He exited the corridor, unrolled the newspaper and put it back on the officer's desk. "You done with your crap yet, Lou?"

"Just waiting for you," the officer said as he walked down the stairs and toward the desk. "Thanks for the break."

North gave a nod and walked in the direction the officer had just come. Lou looked down at his paper, straightened it as best he could and went back to the crossword.

Back up in the squad room, North called the switchboard, the supervisor answered. "Hey Midge, any calls while I was out?"

"None. I hate to ask, but are you any closer to finding Sylvia?" her voice betrayed her fear.

"Not yet, but we'll find her Midge." He hung up the phone and hoped he sounded more confident to her than he did in his own head.

# Chapter 6

North sat at his desk for a moment and tried to put the past three days into perspective. He suddenly ceased his mulling, pulled on his jacket, crushed the worn Bradmore onto his head and began walking toward the door. He stopped, turned around and grabbed the keys to the Belair from his desk before making his way to the parking lot.

The Chevy turned over with a satisfying roar. He slipped the gear shift into drive and pulled out onto Main. With the exception of the Liberty Theatre that had a line out front buying tickets to "The Bridge Over the River Kwai," and a patron walking out of the Trophy Room, the city seemed vacant; only lights in the apartments above some of the shops belied the existence of others. North turned onto M-11 and began driving down the coast.

The evening breeze coming in off of Lake Michigan and through the open windows was welcome after the stifling day. The dust of the day gave way to the smell of moist air as he pulled off the road and onto the lane in the Mere where they'd found De Luca seven hours earlier.

He parked the car where he'd found it and, using his pocket knife, jimmied the door open. He found his way into the kitchen and turned on the fluorescent lamp above the sink; its hum added to the sound of the crickets outside. In all other ways the world seemed unnaturally quiet. He opened the door of the Frigidaire and found four bottles of Falstaff beer, a log of hard salami and a partially eaten loaf of bread.

North was at the table, sitting where De Luca had sat, drinking his beer, eating his food, trying to get into the mobster's head. "Where would he have taken Syl? Why wouldn't he just have brought her here?" The thought vanished as the ringing of the telephone brought him back into the moment.

He walked over to the black wall phone and picked up the receiver, "Yeah," he answered.

"Where the fuck you been? I've been tryin' to reach you for two hours! You was supposed to call me and let me know how the transaction went."

"Uh, there were some unexpected, uh, complications."

"What the fuck you talkin' about, complications? What kind of complications?"

"Well, the big complication is that De Luca got himself shot in the head."

"What?! Who the hell am I talkin' to? What d'you mean De Luca got shot?"

"I had to put a bullet in his head when he wouldn't take directions."

"Who the fuck is this?! Do you know who the fuck you're talkin' to? I ain't someone you want to fuck with."

"I think I'm talking to Lucky Como."

"Yeah, and I think I'm talking to a dead man, that's what I think."

"I'm in your house. I'm eating your food, driving your car. My feet are on your table. You think I'm scared of you? Hell, I take shits bigger than you are."

"I'm gonna find you and I'm gonna kill you. D'you understand what I'm sayin'?"

"Blow it out your ass, Como. You better hope you find me before I find you or your lieutenants are going to be arguing about how they're going to divvy up your organization." North slammed the receiver down as Como began a retort.

Finishing the beer, he walked out of the house and down the lane another eighth-mile to the beach. Wooden stairs led down the bluff some twenty feet to the sandy shore. Moonlight reflected off the water that was gently rolling onto the sand, and beach grass rustled as it was constantly rearranged by a steady breeze. On the horizon, he could see a freighter heading north after having dropped iron ore off at the steel mills in Gary.

He sat for a while on the bottom step and listened to the water rush onto and then fall away from the beach in a gentle rhythm. Looking down the coast he saw a bonfire burning perhaps a mile away. The still was broken by the sound of a twin-engine plane, probably heading to Chicago out of Lakeland.

North stood, climbed back up the bluff and walked to the Chevy. He eased it down the lane and had it parked behind the Safety Building some twenty minutes later.

Back at the Swanson he collected his dry cleaning and mail and threw them both onto the bed. He pulled off his shirt and the cork out of the Old Quaker, swallowing a shot before putting it back on the table.

He eased out of the t-shirt he was wearing and looked at his bandaged ribs in the mirror. The white bandage was now as yellowed as the wallpaper in his room. He splashed some water on his face and, tossing the dry cleaning onto the chair, stretched out on the bed. He fell into a restless sleep thinking that Sylvia was out there somewhere, alone.

## Chapter 7

he July sun was surprisingly excruciating at eight in the morning
and the bandages about North's ribs were already moist from his
Tperspiration. He and Tiffin were standing at the coffee urn in the
corner of the detective's squad room. Brown liquid popped into the
glass percolator top in one-second intervals which told North that the
brew was about complete.

"Let me get this straight," Tiffin said as he stuffed a bite of doughnut
into his mouth, crumbs of which cascaded down his starched white
shirt and tie, "you really spoke with Como last night."

"That's right."

"And you pissed him off?"

"Yup, I pissed him off."

"What were you doing at the house anyway?"

"Trying to get into the mind of De Luca; trying to figure out where
he might have taken Sylvia."

"Come up with anything?"

"Not a thing."

Chief Cummings walked in the door as the words were coming out of
Tiffin's mouth, "Come up with what?"

North looked over his shoulder at his boss, "He asked if we are any
closer to finding Sylvia."

"We've cleared over two hundred cottages, we're going to find her Brick," the boss's voice was somehow more compassionate than North had ever heard him. Cummings grabbed the mail out of his pigeon-hole, pushed his way between the detectives, snatched a doughnut, and walked back into his office.

North looked toward Tiffin who was washing the doughnut down with a cup of coffee fresh from the urn; probably the first fresh coffee made this week, "You notice anything strange about the airport manager's office the other day?"

"What do you mean strange?"

"Did you see the picture of the boys on his desk?"

"Sure. So what?"

"Where's the picture of his wife? You have a picture of your kids on your desk, but Kaye is in the shot with them. Why isn't Jaeger's wife in the picture?"

"I don't know. There could be a lot of reasons."

"And he eats his lunch at his desk every day. Like someone who doesn't have a lot of money to spend."

"So, he's frugal. I'm frugal, too."

"No, you're cheap," North dug at his partner, "Why don't we go down to County Records and follow up on a hunch I've got." With that, North pushed the Bradmore onto his head and walked toward the door, Tiffin following at his heels.

An older man in a suit that should have been retired years ago sat on a stool as they entered the Office of Vital Statistics at the County Courthouse, "May I help you, gentlemen?"

"I'm Detective North, this is Detective Tiffin," North flashed the shield on his belt. "Let me ask you a question. Are divorce records filed by date or by name?"

The worker pushed his glasses up his nose, "Well, by name, but cross-referenced by date."

"Great. I'm looking for a divorce record for Mr. Harold Jaeger."

"Do you have the wife's name?"

"Exactly how many Harold Jaeger's do you figure have gotten divorced in Douglas County?"

"Well, there is that. Let me see what I can find." He pushed himself away from the counter and disappeared behind shelving units lined with books. A few minutes later he reappeared and placed a book on the counter. "Here it is, one Mr. Harold Jaeger divorced his wife Dolores in December of '55."

"Do you have a copy of the divorce decree by any chance?" North said impatiently, having expected it to have been brought out instead of just a record book.

"Well, it is public record, but normally we don't make those available for review."

"Normally!" North shot back. Tiffin put a hand on his shoulder and North backed down a bit.

Tiffin looked toward the startled office worker, his hand still on North's shoulder, "Do you suppose two detectives would be here if there was anything normal about the situation?"

"Well, there is that. Let me go find the file."

"Good idea," Tiffin called after him.

As the minutes passed, North lit a cigarette and impatiently opened and closed the lid of his lighter. Its clicking bothered Tiffin who, wisely, kept quiet. As the clerk hurried back into the room the clicking stopped, "Here it is, Jaeger v. Jaeger, December 20, 1955."

"Merry Christmas," North's tone was bitingly sarcastic. The clerk offered only a blank stare.

He and Tiffin split the file between them. North took the final decree while Tiffin searched through the long list of grounds and properties. Looking up from the papers North turned toward his partner, "She took him for everything!"

"Looks like Harold got himself caught in adultery."

"Nice! Is his, uh, friends name listed in the file."

The clerk, who had been listening stood up from the stool he had planted himself on, "Oh, that'll probably be in the transcript of the court case. I'll go get that for you."

"Good idea," Tiffin said as he continued to look through the folder in front of him. "They'd built quite a life together, house pretty well paid off, cars, nice savings account."

"And she got that in exchange for him dipping his meat into some pepper mill? Not sure that's a fair trade," North shook his head.

"That's because you're not married."

"That's why I'm not married."

The clerk returned with a blue legal file, its pages held in place at the top by a metal clip that extended through two holes punched through each page. "Here's the transcript of the hearing. I must ask that you don't remove the pages from the file."

"Got it," North said as he began flipping the pages over the top of the file. He scanned through about half the file when he stopped and put his finger onto the page in front of him, "Constance Williams."

Tiffin made a note on his pad, "Thanks for your time. I suppose you've got to put all this back now."

"Well, there is that."

Back in the squad room, the two detectives began going through City Directories for LaSalle Harbor as well as some of the outlying towns looking for Miss Williams. Neither found anything.

"What was the Brunette's name at the airport the other morning?" North asked his partner.

"You don't remember? You're the one she was breathing heavy all over. Wasn't it like Susan?"

North flipped through his notebook, "Suzette!" he said mostly to himself, then picking up the phone, "This is Detective North, get me the ticket counter at Lakeland."

"Right away, detective."

A few moments later the phone was answered with a familiar breathy voice, "Lakeland Airport."

"Suzette, this is Detective North."

"Brick!" if anything her voice became even breathier as she spoke his name, then in a lower voice, "I gave you my personal number, I'm surprised you're calling me at work."

"This is business, doll. Your boss got a divorce a couple of years ago, right?"

"Yes, six months or so after I started working here."

"He was involved with a woman, someone by the name of Constance Williams. Do you know who she is?"

"Connie? Sure, I remember her. She was here frequently until right after the divorce."

"What did she look like?"

"Platinum blonde, five-five or so, heavy on the makeup and wore too much Estée Lauder Youth Dew; you could smell her coming before she got into the building.

"You say she stopped coming in, like right after she found out Jaeger didn't have any more money to spend on her?" North said mostly to himself.

"I wouldn't doubt that. Men like Mr. Jaeger aren't very attractive when their billfold is flat, if you know what I mean. Now, men like you on the other hand..."

North cut her off, "You have any idea where we could find Constance or Connie?"

"If I recall, it seems like I heard her say that she lived up around Crystal Springs, but I could be wrong."

"That's a good place to start. I owe you one!"

"I'm going to call in that marker, Brick."

North hung up the receiver and looked at Tiffin who had been straining to hear the other side of the conversation. "She tells us to look around Crystal Springs."

"Crystal Springs? Holy shit, that's all unincorporated up there, not going to be easy finding our missing mistress in farm country."

"Shouldn't be too hard to find a platinum blonde wearing too much makeup and expensive perfume."

They checked with both the Department of Motor Vehicles and the Department of Taxation and Revenue. They came up with some two dozen Constance or Connie Williams living in Michigan. None of them in Douglas County. "Doesn't mean she isn't living in Crystal Springs," Tiffin said as he looked over the legal pad full of addresses.

"No, it doesn't. Also, it doesn't have to be her real name either."

"Well, if it isn't then we're up shit creek."

"Won't be the first time," North added as his partner looked over the legal pad yet again. "I think it's about time we go and have another chat with Mr. Jaeger."

The Ford was stifling when they got in it. North peeled off his jacket and threw it and his hat onto the backseat. They turned onto Main and were at the airport inside of ten minutes. "You occupy the brunette with some questions about our Miss Williams, I want a chance to talk with Jaeger alone."

"You sure that's wise?"

"I don't think Suzette is going to jump you if that's what you mean."

"No, do you think you should talk to Jaeger alone?"

"I'm going to screw with his mind for a few minutes. Maybe he'll offer something we can use. I just don't want to be interrupted. So, you keep our brunette occupied and keep anyone from wondering back to the boss's office."

"Got it."

They pulled up next to the terminal under as much shade as North could find. The covered area where they parked on Monday being occupied by a baggage cart. North pulled on his brown suit jacket and crushed the Bradmore onto his mop of sweaty hair. Tiffin straightened his tie as they walked into the terminal building.

Suzette had one round hip balanced on a stool behind the ticket counter. She jumped up as the two detectives entered. "Brick, er Detective North! How can I help you?"

"My partner has a few questions for you. I'm going to find the men's room." He said without ever breaking stride. Tiffin pulled a notepad and pencil from his jacket pocket and placed them on the counter. He began asking questions such as her full name and address as North turned down the corridor to Jaeger's office. He entered without knocking and caught the airport manager by surprise, "Jaeger," he said in a harsh tone.

"What!" Jaeger jumped a few inches out of his chair, "Um, what can I do for you detective?"

North walked behind the desk and stood over him, "I don't like to be lied to Jaeger. And I think you're lying to me."

"I've answered every question truthfully!" He argued back.

"Just not the whole truth, right pal?" The detective said as he pushed the back of the swivel chair, forcing the airport manager to look up at him.

"I don't know what you're talking about."

"Sure, you do. When my partner and I were in her on Monday you forgot to tell us some things, didn't you?" North pretended to know something that he didn't.

"Like what?"

"Like why don't you start with what we both know you omitted from your story."

Jaeger shifted his weight in the chair and brought his feet back down to the floor. "I didn't omit anything!" He shouted.

"Come on, Jaeger, you're sweating like a pig, you're breathing hard, and you won't look me in the eye. You're lying. I know that and so do you. Now, tell me what you're lying about."

"I can't. I've got nothing to say."

"That's two different things," North grabbed Jaeger by the knot of his tie and pulled him up slightly from the chair, "you can't, or you won't?"

"I can't tell you what I don't know."

"And you won't tell me what you do." North released his grip on Jaeger's tie and the man's butt dropped two inches into the swivel chair. "Let's try talking about something you do know about. Tell me about Constance Williams."

"Connie? I haven't seen her in eighteen months."

"I didn't ask when you last saw her; I asked you to tell me about her."

"She worked for Michigan Vending at their office. We used to buy from them and I met her there. Guess we kind of hit it off right away."

"Go on."

"Well, she and I dated for a while but we broke up."

"That's after the former Mrs. Jaeger kicked your ass out the front door."

Outraged the airport manager pushed himself out of his chair, "My personal life has nothing to do with this."

"Sit down before I sit you down!" North barked. "Your personal life has everything to do with this." Jaeger plopped back into the chair. "Where does Constance Williams live?"

"I have no idea. She used to live off of Cass Road in Crystal Springs, but she isn't there anymore. I went up there last fall looking to see if we could patch things up and she'd moved."

"Where off of Cass Road?"

"Mill Creek, quarter-mile down. There's a tourist cabin court. She was in number three."

"I'm not done with you yet, Jaeger. You and I have a lot more to talk about and next time we meet you're going to do a lot more talking." With that North turned and walked down the corridor to the lobby.

"Come on, Tiff, we've got people to see." Tiffin straightened up and thanked Suzette for her time.

"You gonna call me, Brick?" She said in a frustrated voice as they pushed the doors open.

"Don't worry, doll," he called back to her. To his partner he said, "what'd you learn from the brunette?"

"That she has a lot of questions about you. What you learn from Jaeger?"

"That he's lying about something and the Williams woman works for Michigan Vending."

The two detectives stopped at a gas station and used the pay phone to call the Safety Building. The dime dropped into the coin return as he finished dialing the last digit. "This is Detective North, get me an address for Michigan Vending."

North recorded the information and they drove to the south side of town. Michigan Vending was a red brick warehouse with a half dozen bays for delivery vans and an office door facing the street with a tattered canvas awning doing a miserable job of blocking the late morning sun.

They walked in to a small common office area housing three desks each occupied by a sweaty middle-aged man. No sign of an attractive blonde in sight. The detectives stood there for a couple of minutes while the men took or made calls.

"Hey Tiff," North said in a loud voice, "these boys think we're Claud Rains."

"What?"

"The Invisible Man."

One of the men looked up from his desk, "Is there something I can help you with?"

Tiffin responded, "You can tell us where to find Constance Williams."

"Like I've told every one of you bill collectors, she ain't worked here in over a year."

North flashed his gold shield and a big grin, "We're not bill collectors and I don't like your attitude."

"That badge doesn't impress me, buddy. Like I said, Connie hasn't worked here in over a year. But her name comes up often enough she might as well still be here."

"How's that?" North said as he stared down at the man who was a good head shorter than he was.

"We got a steady stream of bill collectors and what-not looking for her. She musta owed money to half the state."

"You got an address for her on file?"

"Nah, I don't hang onto stuff I don't need. She lived up around Crystal Springs."

"That's a twenty-five-mile drive from here. She make that drive every day?" Tiffin asked incredulously.

"I doubt it. She usually found someone who would put her up for the night, if you know what I mean."

"I think we've got the idea," then to his partner, "come on Tiff, let's make a drive up to Crystal Springs."

The drive took nearly forty minutes and the midday sun was baking the Ford and its occupants. Cass Road was the main route and it wasn't hard to locate Mill Creek Road. As Jaeger had said, Benton's Tourist Court was less than a quarter-mile off Cass. Twelve small cottages sat in a semi-circle surrounded by old-growth oaks. Once out of the car they could hear the springs burbling over rocks behind the property. The cabin closest to the street had a sign noting it as the office. As they approached an older woman swung the screen door open.

"We're full up."

"Good afternoon," Tiffin offered, "we're not looking for a room, just some information about a former resident."

Looking at their dusty car and then to them she said, "You boys policemen or something?"

"We're with the LaSalle Harbor police. My name if Tiffin, this is Detective North."

"Mind if I see your badges?"

Both detectives pushed their coats back revealing the badges on their belts.

"Thank you, can't be too cautious. Now, who exactly are you looking for?"

"Constance Williams," North said.

"Shoulda guessed. She owes me a month and a half rent. Just packed up and left in the middle of the night. Sheriff said there wasn't anything they could do. Why are you looking for her?"

"We've got a few questions to ask her."

Tiffin added, "and if we find her, we could charge her with skipping out on her bill with you."

"That would be most kind if you could. The income from here is all I've got now that my Jack passed on."

North looked perturbed, "So, you've got no idea where she might have gone?"

"Not a lick. She left in a hurry, but I've still got a valise she left behind. You can have it if you want."

"That would be very helpful, Ma'am," North said, tipping his hat in her direction. As she stepped back into the office, he looked at his partner, "Why'd you tell her we could charge Williams for skipping on her bill?"

"Thought if I threw that in, she might be more helpful."

"Good thinking, partner. You just might be a good detective someday," he said with a grin.

"Thanks for your support," Tiffin started to say as the landlady came back out with a worn brown leather valise, the initials CAW embossed on the side.

"You're welcome," she said with a smile.

"Pardon me," Tiffin looked at her questioningly.

"You're welcome for my support. I'm glad to help. I've written down my name and telephone number should you get my money for me."

"Thank you very much, Missus," he looked at the piece of paper, "Benton. We'll be in touch."

He threw the valise into the back seat as North slipped behind the steering wheel. "Aren't you curious about what's in the case?" he asked as the Ford turned onto the main road and back toward town.

"Sure, but it'll wait until we're back at the squad room and can carefully note the contents."

They checked the car back into the motor pool and within several minutes had a table cleared off in the squad room. A couple of officers leaned against the wall as North forced the lock of the case open with his knife.

"Ooh," one of the officers laughed as North pulled out a sheer nightie, "what other treasures you come up with, Detective?" He was answered with a bra thrown at his face.

"Not much, Davidson, but you might look cute in that."

"Ha, ha, very funny," Davidson said as a blush rose on his cheeks and his fellow officer chuckled at him.

In the corner of the case were a few envelopes held together with a rubber band. Tiffin grabbed the stack while North laid the rest of the clothes out on the table, "Let's see what we've got here. Bill from a hat shop in Detroit, bill from a dry cleaner in Muskegon," and as an aside, "this girl gets around. Hey, here's something. I've got a letter addressed to Williams from a Mrs. Janice Shoemaker on Catalpa Lane here in town."

"Well, don't stand there, open it up!" North exclaimed.

"Let's see, Dear Connie, uh, some stuff about getting together for someone's birthday. It's signed Aunt Jan."

"I think we should see if Miss Shoemaker still lives on Catalpa."

Tiffin was already putting his hat on, "I'm already out the door."

# Chapter 8

S ylvia was awakened from a troubled sleep by the sound of a nearby train whistle. Heavy steel wheels clacked out their rhythm as they bounced over seams in the tracks.

The room was hot and humid, the air stifling, and rough sisal ropes dug into her wrists and ankles where they secured her to a heavy wooden armchair. The more she struggled, the more they cut into her flesh. In one attempt to free herself, she had almost managed to tip the chair over but managed to balance herself before she fell on her head.

What parts of her that weren't covered by clothing were covered by fly bites. None of that was as important as the fact that her throat was so dry that she could no longer call out for help. She had never known thirst like this. "How long before someone comes for me?" she sobbed, but neither words nor tears escaped.

"What would Brick do?" she thought to herself. He'd have an answer; he always did. "Oh Brick, why didn't I listen to you?"

# Chapter 9

Five Forty-Seven Catalpa was less than a mile from the Safety building and North and Tiffin were there within minutes of leaving their desks. The wooden steps leading up to the screen porch were worn, but the house was tidy and the lawn well kept.

Tiffin pushed the button and the two-note bell rang deep inside the frame house. "Coming," a woman's voice sounded as the figure of a middle-aged woman appeared in the door. "Oh, gentlemen, how may I help you?"

"Ma'am, I'm Detective Tiffin, this is Detective North, are you Janice Shoemaker?"

"Why, yes I am. Is there some problem?"

"Ma'am," Tiffin asked as he pulled his hat from his head, "May we come inside?"

"Well, I don't see why not. My Bert's upstairs napping, he works nights at Michigan Canners."

"We'll try not to wake him," North said as he followed Mrs. Shoemaker and Tiffin inside to an immaculate living room.

"Now, what can I do for you?" she said as she crossed her ankles and perched herself on the edge of a small armchair.

North looked toward his partner and then to the lady of the house, "We're actually trying to speak with your niece, Constance Williams."

"Oh, Lord! What has Connie gotten herself into this time?" the exasperation showed in her voice.

Tiffin settled into a Barcalounger, "We don't know that she's in any trouble, Mrs. Shoemaker. Actually, we're just trying to get some background on a man she may have known."

"Forgive me, Detectives. I don't mean to speak ill of my brother's daughter, but Connie has probably known a number of men."

"When's the last time you saw your niece, Mrs. Shoemaker?" North asked as he took in the room.

"Do call me Janice."

"Okay, Janice, when's the last time you saw your niece?"

"Oh, that's got to be last year May. She came in looking for train fare to Chicago and enough to get into a hotel room for a couple of nights. Said she had a job lined up and she'd be able to pay me back real quick."

"Did you give her the money?"

"Gave her almost forty dollars that I'd squirreled away. Oh, don't tell Bert, he'd be furious!"

"Don't worry, we won't," Tiffin offered.

North continued, "Have you heard from her since?"

"Got a postcard from her last summer; it's around here somewhere," she said as she stood and began looking through some items on the edge of the mantle. She handed a card to North, "Here it is."

North looked briefly at the photo on the front of the card. It looked like every other motel postcard he'd ever seen; an image of a room with a couple of beds, the interior of a coffee shop, and a pool. He quickly flipped it over and looked at the return address. "Shawnee Motor Court, Crawford Avenue, Skokie, Illinois." At Skokie, he looked at Tiffin. "What are the odds, Tiff?"

"Odds?" Mrs. Shoemaker asked.

"Skokie keeps coming up, ma'am," Tiffin answered.

"Mind if we keep this card, Mrs. Shoemaker?" North asked even as he was sliding it into his pocket.

"No, not at all. Is Connie in trouble?"

"We hope not ma'am," North said as he stood, "we hope not."

Back in the car, the two drove past the High School and down to the Fifth Wheel for lunch. "You know, Tiff," North said as pushed meatloaf and mashed potatoes around with his fork, "we grabbed up a pound of smack. Somebody's got to be hurting trying to get their next hit."

"I bet they are. So, what are you suggesting?"

"I'm suggesting that users may be getting desperate enough to be open to talking if we let them know we have what they need."

"You suggesting that we give them heroin?" Tiffin said in a voice loud enough that the other patrons turned toward him.

"We can't give them any, but they don't know that, do they?" North looked down at the plate in front of him and pushed it away.

"You need to eat something," Tiffin offered in a quiet voice, not wanting to anger his partner.

"Not hungry. The only thing I want is to find Syl and help Lucky Como into the next life."

"They'll find her, Brick. They're clearing cottages and I understand that the Sheriff's added deputies to the search."

"Red can't find his ass with both hands and his deputies would have trouble investigating a tractor versus cow accident."

North pushed himself from the table and grabbed the Bradmore from the chair next to the one he had been sitting on. "Let's go talk to some junkies."

Tiffin put three silver dollars on the counter next to the register and smiled at the young waitress "Keep it," he said as they walked out trying to keep up with North who already had the car running when he got there.

"So where are we doing this junkie hunt?" he asked as he slid into the passenger seat.

"I'm thinking the Flats would probably be a good place to start," North pushed the gear shift into first and let the clutch out. The Ford found its way into traffic and down toward what the locals called "the Flats," which was the flood plain where the river would overflow before the dams were built upstream. Now it housed low rent apartments, small shops, and bars, all for the most part owned by negroes.

North and Tiffin pulled up to the curb in front of a small grocery store that also sold beer. A group of men hid their malt liquor bottles behind their backs as the detectives got out and walked towards them.

"We don't give a shit about the beer," North said. "We're just here to let you know that we scored a pound of good smack from Lucky Como's gang and will trade a hit for information."

A large man eyed the detectives up and down, "We ain't got nothin' to say," with that, the spokesman took a deep draw from the bottle he was holding, which gave permission to the other men to do the same.

North looked him over. The man was about his age, heavier by maybe twenty pounds with hands that did not look like he used them for a living. A tattoo of a skull pierced by a knife was easily seen over his dark skin. Even with the rough exterior, he saw a familiar bearing. "What branch you serve in during the war?"

"What's it to you?"

"It just looks like you've seen some real shit. I respect a man who's seen the crap the world offers and still holds himself upright."

"Hear that, boys? He says he's got respect for me!" Easy laughter erupted from the group. He turned back to the detectives. "Whadya boys want?"

Stepping a little closer North lowered his voice, "We don't want to jack anyone up, just trying to get a little information. If you know anyone who knows anyone, they just have to ask for Detective North."

"I'll pass that along."

Tiffin slid into the passenger seat and had barely gotten the door shut when North let the clutch out and the Ford lurched forward, "You in a hurry?"

"Something just occurred to me that I haven't considered."

"What's that?"

"As much as the junkies are looking to score a hit of Como's smack, how much more does he want it back?"

"Yeah, I bet he does."

"So, we just put the word on the street that we're giving his shit away. Somehow I think that's going to piss ol' Lucky off more than us just taking it." They followed River Front road up to Main and headed back to the Safety Building. "Let's see if young Mr. Bryant is willing to talk about where he got his smack from."

"He would've gotten it from De Luca, wouldn't he?"

"No, we know that De Luca had his own personal stash and the brick in the car. We know that De Luca gave him twenty dollars for kidnapping Syl. When we found Bryant he had heroin, but he didn't have any money on him. He bought those drugs from someone; let's find out who."

The ambulance belonging to the Kerlikowske Funeral Home was behind the Safety Building when they arrived. Doc Howard was talking to the driver as the detectives approached, "Get him back to the morgue, I'll be right behind you."

"Doc!" North shouted over the sound of the mammoth Cadillac as it pulled away, "what the hell is going on?"

"Prisoner hanged himself, wasn't discovered until it was too late."

North and Tiffin looked at each other, North kicked at the gravel, "Fucking son of a bitch!"

"Who was it, doc?" Tiffin asked even though in his heart he knew the answer.

"Billy Bryant. Tied the blanket around his neck and the bars of his cell and stepped off the bunk. Didn't break his neck, but asphyxiated himself."

North stepped up, "He strangled himself?"

"Probably dope-sick."

"How's that?" Tiffin asked.

"The brain gets used to the way the drugs affect it, and it adapts so that it can function. Withdrawal happens when the brain isn't getting what it needs. Depending upon the amount of drugs like heroin the brain has gotten used to, withdrawal can be terrible to go through."

Tiffin took off his fedora and scratched his head, "So suicide is better than the pain?"

"It's a way out from the pain. Now if you excuse me, I've got an ambulance to meet."

"Son of a bitch!" North repeated. "If he wasn't fucking dead, I'd kill him myself."

Inside they immediately went down to the cells. A young officer was being questioned by the Chief, "I wasn't gone but five minutes, I don't know how this could have happened."

Chief Cummings looked deep into the officer's eyes, "You shouldn't have been gone at all! If you needed to fucking relieve yourself you call for help and you wait until someone comes down here before you leave."

"My girl was dropping off some dinner and couldn't wait."

"She could have left it at the Sergeant's desk for you!"

"I guess I wanted to see her for a minute."

The Chief's voice was getting hoarse from yelling, "I guess you wanted to get your nuts off! Go home, I'm giving you a week off without pay, let's see if that helps you figure out what head you're going to think with!" The officer lowered his head and began to climb the stairs. Cummings looked toward the detectives who were standing there, "What?! You think I was too hard on him?"

North, hands balled into fists in his pants pockets, spoke first, "Not as hard as I would be if I was the boss. I'da fucking fired him…"

"… or worse," Tiffin interjected, "sent him to the fire department!" The mood was suddenly less tense.

"You boys come up with anything?"

"Gotta lot of pieces to the puzzle, but don't know how they quite fit together," North, finally relaxing, said.

The chief, also relaxing, pulled his pipe from his jacket pocket, filled the bowl with tobacco and, lighting a match, carefully lit the tobacco and pulled the smoke into his mouth, "So, what have you got?"

North lit a Pall Mall, "Got word out to the junkie community that we've got smack in exchange for information. Followed a lead to the airport manager's former girlfriend and found that she's hooked up with Skokie, and probably Como. Was just coming in to find out who Bryant was buying his drugs from."

Smoke issued from the corner of the chief's mouth, "Guess that dirty little secret is going to the grave with Bryant. Go talk with people he hung out with and see if he's got any family. Guess we need to tell someone he's dead."

The detectives did a search of Douglas County records and came up with nothing on Billy Bryant. Tiffin found a birth record for a William A. Bryant, born January 11, 1939, in Cass County, just thirty miles away. "Be about the right age as our Billy,"

North swung around in his chair, "Next of kin?"

"Father, James Bryant, died in the war. Mother Frances nee O'Brian, killed in a car accident two years ago."

"Fine, so we got a dead junkie orphan. Let's go talk with his pals."

It was late in the afternoon we they arrived at the pool hall. The place was getting crowded with blue-collar workers, but the little clutch of greasers from their previous visit was occupying a corner booth. One of them displayed a shiner in the shape of North's left knuckles.

Tiffin spoke first, "My friend here," giving a nod toward North, "would like to beat the shit out of all of you. I convinced him that you would be cooperative. But let's be honest, he doesn't think you know how to cooperate, and frankly, neither do I."

The one with the knuckle tattoo kept his head down. "What the fuck do you coppers want?" offered the newest leader.

"Well first," Tiffin began, "we wanted to offer our condolences on the death of your pal, Billy." At his words, the gang became visibly shaken. "Seems your pal decided the hang himself this afternoon."

"Yeah, well, he was a dip stick anyway," offered their leader.

North broke his silence, "So, since we can't ask Billy any questions, we're going to ask you instead."

"We're not going to say anything, are we boys?" their leader asked as North put his hand on the back of the youth's head and slammed his face into the tabletop. Blood immediately began to flow from an obviously broken nose. North grabbed a towel from the bar and handed it to the boy.

"What's wrong with you?! Getting blood all over the table? Wipe that up!" Then to the group, "Who did Bryant buy his smack from?" The boys all looked away, North put his hand hard against one of the other boy's head.

"Alright, I'll tell you," the lad shouted. "I'll tell you, just don't hurt me."

"I'm glad you're willing to be cooperative," then to Tiffin, "Get the door, let's step outside." North, his grip tight around the back of

116

youth's neck, pushed him through the door. The pool hall was as quiet as a convent as they walked out.

Tiffin let the door shut behind them, "My partner here," nodding to North, "isn't as patient as I am, before your nose ends up on the other side of your head, maybe you should start talking."

"Billy gets, er, got it from this guy called Snake."

"Snake got another name?" North said through gritted teeth.

"I don't know. He's an old guy like you, but he's colored."

Tiffin cut him off, "What does he look like?"

"Big guy, he's got a tattoo on his arm," the kid placed his left palm on his right arm showing where the ink was.

North relaxed his gripped slightly, "What's the tattoo of?"

"I don't know, a knife stuck in a skull or something."

North stared at Tiffin for a moment. "Fuck!" he shouted loud enough that his syllable echoed off nearby walls. "Get the hell out of here," he said as he pushed the teen away.

They took a moment and used the payphone in the pool hall and caught the Chief up on what was going on. "We're going back down to Goulka's Grocery where we saw him earlier today," Tiffin shouted over the din.

Cummings rubbed the top of his head and neck, "You two see if you can find him. In the meantime I think I'll send the paddy wagon to the

Flats and see if we can't sweep up a few undesirables who might know something."

By early evening the sweep of the Flats had loaded the four cells in the Safety Building with a dozen occupants most of whom had been picked up for vagrancy, drinking in public, or in some cases, just being outside.

"What're we being held for?" One of the incarcerated yelled from the cell block.

Lou looked up from the newspaper where, until he was interrupted, he had been diligently working on today's crossword, "They don't tell me that kind of stuff," he shouted back toward the cells, "they just tell me to make sure I lock the doors before I leave you."

"This is wrong," the voice called back, "you can't arrest us for being outside."

"Unless you know a seven-letter word meaning a perplexing situation, there's nothing to talk about."

"Problem," replied the voice.

"And that's what you've got," Lou said as he tried without luck to fit the offered word into the puzzle.

"Mystery," said North as he came down the steps.

"Hey, that's it! Thanks."

North tossed his hat on the coat tree that stood near the desk, "and a mystery is what we've got. Seems like our Mr. Snake has up and disappeared on us. Any of these gents seem like they want to talk?"

Lou stood up and went to the steel barred door that led into the cell corridor. "Hey crossword guy, you wanna talk to the detective?"

"If it gets me out of here, yes," came the reply.

A slight young man in his early twenties was led into the small interrogation room near the cells. He was clothed in a pressed white shirt with a narrow black tie, grey slacks and perfectly shined shoes. North fanned the guard away as he began to handcuff the young man to the table, "I don't think that'll be necessary," he said toward Lou and then to the young man, "Do you?"

"No sir," came the quick reply.

"What's your name?" Tiffin asked as he flipped his spiral pad open.

"James Wilson, sir."

"And what were you doing that you were arrested for?" North asked as he flipped his lighter closed.

"Waiting for a ride to Memorial Hospital."

"You sick?" North asked as he blew smoke toward the lone light bulb on the ceiling.

"No sir, I'm working there this summer before I head back to school in September."

"Working at what, exactly?"

"I'm working as an orderly."

Tiffin looked up from the notes he had been jotting, "Where's this school you're going to?"

"University of Michigan, I'll be entering my first year of medical school."

"Medical school?" North couldn't hide his surprise, "You gonna be a doctor or something?"

"You surprised a colored man can be a doctor?"

"Well, I guess I am."

"To be honest, I guess I'm a little surprised I was accepted, even though I graduated in the top ten percent of the class of '57."

"So, we're looking for a man goes by the name of Snake. Big guy, probably around thirty-five, over six foot. Know who we're talking about?"

"Sure, that'd be Sam Nelson. He stays on Tenth, a couple of blocks up from Gray. He's been shaking down folks for protection money for a long time."

"This Nelson, he sell drugs as well as protection, does he?"

"He'd sell his grandmother if he could make a few dollars on her."

"You've been very helpful," Tiffin reassured the young man, "I think we can let you go." North gave a nod toward his partner.

"No, sir," Wilson retorted, "you let me go and some of those other guys will know I snitched. You put me back and question a few others or I'll end up hurt, or worse."

North and the older officer led him back to the cells and pushed him into one where two others were sitting on a bunk. The detective yelled,

"Fine, you won't talk, let's see if your friend here will." With that Lou grabbed one of the other men and they slammed the cell door.

After interviewing three more men about a fictitious liquor store robbery, they let those without warrants go, including Wilson.

Tiffin whispered as he passed, "good luck on that doctor thing."

"Thank you," Wilson whispered back.

# Chapter 10

T he sun had gone down, but twilight would last until ten o'clock at this time or year. The temperature wasn't cooperating; it was going to be another hot night. Tiffin had gone home for the evening leaving North alone in the office.

Cummings walked out of his office, "Red's boys," he said referring to the Sheriff, "have helped us make a dent on the cottages. We're down to maybe a few dozen that haven't been checked."

North paced the squad room, "You know I want to be out there!"

"And the people in hell want iced tea," the chief retorted. "I need you to figure out these two murders. The mayor is on my ass, says it's bad for the tourist trade."

"Fuck the tourists, and fuck the mayor too for that matter," North fumed. "She's been out there for two days in God only knows what kind of conditions."

"We're going to find her."

"I want to make sure we find her alive!" North said as he grabbed his coat and pushed his fedora onto his mop of hair.

"Where you going?" the chief shouted behind him.

"Out!" came the reply from the stairwell.

North walked into the officer's locker room on the first floor. His ribs ached, he was tired and he didn't remember when he'd eaten last. A handful of officers were taking their uniforms off and putting on their civvies. "Okay, who's been trying to locate our missing switchboard operator?"

"I've been out a couple times," one of the younger officers responded.

"You familiar with the area that's being searched most recently?"

"Up north there's some older cottages north of Watervliet around a small lake off Hagar Shores and Becht roads. And a few on the north side of Little Paw Paw Lake."

"Grab your gear, you and I are about to take a road trip."

"I gotta clear that with the Sarge."

"I'll take care of your Sergeant, just grab your gear."

"Yes, sir!" the young officer responded with a mixture of excitement and fear.

North grabbed the Ford keys from the pegboard near the backdoor. He got to the car first, the younger man wrestling to get into his Sam Brown belt as he ran. "What's your name?" North asked as he pushed the car into first.

"Brodeur, sir."

"How about a first name?"

"Will."

"I'm Detective North," the detective extended his hand.

"I know who you are, sir," he responded.

"That good or bad?"

"Oh, ah, good sir."

"Ha! Okay, you be navigator, can you get me to that first little lake you were talking about?"

"Sure, keep north on M-63 for about ten miles, then take Hagar Shores Road inland about two miles. Becht will be on the right, then south."

North turned the car onto Main and headed out of town. The two rode in silence for most the twenty minute trip, although Brodeur had a thousand questions he wanted to ask.

"Turn here!" Brodeur shouted suddenly.

"Dammit," North shouted as he turned the wheel while stepping down on the clutch and brake, "give me a little more warning next time." The Ford fishtailed a bit and gravel flew up behind them. With a goal in sight, he sped down the narrow country road. Neither he nor the young officer saw the railroad crossing sign on the side of the road as it curved up and to the right.

A their headlights swept over a stand of trees, North caught sight of a stalled train in just enough time to stop the car before it hit the small incline up to the tracks.

"I'm sorry, sir," Brodeur said, "I didn't hear a train."

"We didn't hear it because it's not moving."

"Should we wait for it to move?" the officer asked.

"Could be here for hours. Let's head over to Little Paw Paw." North executed a perfect three point turn and the Ford lurched back to the main road. Within fifteen minutes they were on the road that looped around Little Paw Paw Lake. He and the officer used the spotlights mounted on either side of the windshield to search for cottages. A thousand feet down the road they began to find their targets. A number of them were occupied with light and music spilling out.

"What about any of these?" Brodeur inquired.

"I doubt there's a party going on wherever they're keeping Sylvia."

"Do you expect that she's going to be alone?"

"I don't know what to expect. But if she's on this road I don't think they'd put her next to anything that's occupied."

The drove further down the road and found a cottage by itself that didn't seem to be occupied. More to himself than to Brodeur, North said, "Faded white siding, just like Bryant said." He grabbed a flashlight from the glovebox and turned the car and its lights off.

With a finger to his lips, he motioned the officer to follow him. Keeping low, they quietly approached the cottage. The only thing they could hear was the chirping of crickets and the humming of cicadas. North approached a window on the right side of the house. He cautiously looked in, but curtains prevented him from seeing what lay beyond. The two made their way around the back side of the house that faced the lake. Two worn wooden steps led up to a small porch which was devoid of any furniture. The backdoor had boards nailed over it. It looked like it had been closed for many years.

They circled around the far side of the house and found curtains also blocked his view into the windows. On the street side he approached the front door, boards which had been pulled from the door, lay on the porch. North tried the door, but it was locked. Without hesitation, his large foot kicked the door open. It bounced off a wall on the inside and swung shut. North blocked it with his shoulder.

"Uh, detective, that's breaking and entering," Brodeur said through his shock.

"So arrest me, officer." North replied as he flicked on the flashlight and stepped inside, gun in hand. "Sylvia!" he shouted, even though it was obvious the small cottage was unoccupied.

The pair investigated four more cottages. At two they awoke residents. The other two were as empty as the first, just not in as bad of repair.

"What now, sir?"

"Let's see if that trains moved."

"It's after midnight, do you want to try again in the morning?"

"Like hell," the detective said in a rough voice. "We're this far, let's keep looking. Unless you've got somewhere better to be, 'cuz I can drop you off and you can hitchhike back to town."

Brodeur put his head down, "Oh, no sir. I'm good."

"Good," was the only thing North said as they swung back to toward Becht. They cautiously rounded the curve to find the train had moved on. The Ford bounced over the tracks with enough force that Brodeur was certain they had probably broken a spring.

"There should be a dirt road to the left up ahead. That'll take us to the lake."

North slowed the car down and used his spotlight to light up the side of the road. Eyes glowed momentarily before a pair of raccoons dove into the brush. The road came into view as did a faded sign that read, "Private Lane."

The dirt lane, barely a car length wide, wound to the right. About a quarter mile down they spotted a small white cottage. It was dark and showed obvious signs of neglect. Like most of the cottages they had seen, this one was a single story, narrow and of simple construction. As they stepped out of the car, North once again cautioned his young protégé to be quiet. They approached the porch and the detective slowly put his weight down on the step in an effort to make no sound. It groaned as his full weight was applied. The second and third steps did as well, although not quite as loudly. He crossed the porch and looked into the small window in the door. He couldn't make out anything but what appeared to be the shape of some furniture.

Instead of kicking this door in, he pounded on the door frame, "Police, open the door!" Silence followed. Again he pounded, "Police! We're coming in!"

"Sir, I feel like I need to remind you that we don't have a search warrant."

"Sometimes, kid, you've gotta go with your gut." With that he forced the door open with his shoulder. The old wooden frame gave way with a pop. With the .38 in his left hand and flashlight in the right, he cautiously entered a small room. The air inside was heavy and stale, the yellow orb of light from the flashlight lit up various pieces of furniture.

They crossed into the next room which housed a table, a hutch and a heavy wooden chair. Tied to the chair was a still form. "Sylvia!" he shouted. She did not move.

Dropping to his knees he put his hand on her arm, she was burning up. "Help me get her out of these ropes," he ordered Brodeur who had up to this moment just been staring at the lifeless form in the chair.

"Is she, uh, alive?" he managed to stammer.

"Holy shit," North said as he freed her right arm and leg, "barely, but I can feel her heart beating." He put his hand on her chest, "Damn, it's beating so fast." Brodeur managed to free her left side and North scooped her up in his arms. She seemed small and frail as he carried her to the car.

"You drive," he directed the officer, "I'll stay with her in the backseat." Brodeur opened the driver's side back door and North slid in with Sylvia. He cradled her head in his lap. "Memorial Hospital NOW!"

The young officer turned the key, pushed the ignition button with his toe and ground gears getting the Ford into reverse. He turned on the red light which sat on the dashboard and, with siren blaring, raced into town. Sylvia remained deathly quiet.

"Hang in there, Syl, you're going to be alright," North whispered to her, although he really didn't believe it himself.

While it was only some twenty minutes before the Mainline was pulling up the emergency entrance of the hospital, to North it felt like a lifetime. "Go get some help," he barked.

Moments later Brodeur appeared with a gurney and two orderlies, their white lab coats fluttering behind them as they ran. One of them was familiar. "Wilson," North said, "give me hand and then find Doc Howard."

"Yes sir!," came the reply.

North helped roll the gurney through the double doors and into a white tiled room. Immediately a nurse was cutting away her soiled clothing while a young intern placed his stethoscope on her chest. He shook his head and looked toward the detective, "Is she family?"

"She's a friend, why?"

"We probably need to contact her family, she's is pretty bad shape."

North fought the urge to pull his gun and demand Sylvia be taken care of.

"We've never really spoken about her family," he said instead. "I know she's from Detroit."

"Why don't you go sit down in the waiting room and we'll give her the best care possible," the nurse said as she put her hands on his arm and directed him out of the curtained off room.

He found Brodeur seated in the waiting area. "She gonna be alright?" he asked.

"I don't know," then looking at the young officer, "Why don't you take the car back to the Safety Building? I'll wait here."

"Should I start working on the report when I get there?" he asked, hoping the answer would be no. He got his wish and left North looking out a window with his back to the room.

A few minutes passed before he turned to find a payphone. Dropping a dime into the slot, he called dispatch. "This is Detective North, I need you to wake up the Chief and Detective Tiffin. Get them to Memorial Hospital as quickly as possible."

"Is this about Sylvia?" the operator asked, "Is she okay?"

"It is and I wish I knew," he answered honestly, "I wish I knew."

## Chapter 11

North was just catching the Chief up on the events of the evening when both Tiffin and Doc Howard entered the waiting room from separate entrances.

North looked away from his boss, "Doc?"

"It's not good, Brick," the doctor offered as he pushed his hands into his white coat pockets, "she's extremely dehydrated and not responsive. We couldn't raise a vein to put an IV in, so I had to cut into the subclavian vein," he said as he lifted his right hand to touch his own collarbone, "and even at that it was difficult to get an IV going."

"What's that mean?" North asked.

"It means she's as dehydrated as anyone I've ever treated, even in the war. We've just now got her on IV fluids. I suspect she's lost ten, fifteen percent of her body weight in fluid. As a result, her blood level is very low, and that's caused cardiac arrhythmia."

"Is that why her heart was beating like a bird?"

"That's one way to describe it."

North was pacing as the doctor answered his questions, "And why was she so hot?"

"As you lose fluids, your blood becomes more concentrated and, at some point, it triggers your kidneys to shut down and hold on to what fluid they can find," he took a breath, "Less fluid means that you don't sweat and that can cause your body temperature to rise greatly above normal. Sylvia's temperature was about a hundred and five, so I'm also concerned about the possibility of brain damage."

131

North swung around and kicked an aluminum framed chair over, "Fucking son-of-a-bitch!" The expletive caused a nurse who had been heading toward the waiting room to turn and walk away.

"What're her odds, Doc?" Tiffin asked.

"I'm going to be honest," Howard said in a practiced, soft tone, "they're not good."

North stared at the doctor for a moment, "Thanks Doc, I know you're doing what you can."

Howard reached out and put his hand on the detective's shoulder, "I'll keep you informed." With that, Howard walked toward the corridor he'd come from. Pausing before exiting he turned back, "Want my advice?"

"What's that?" North looked back toward the doctor.

"Go get some sleep. Nothing you can do here tonight."

Looking at his detectives in a paternal manner, the Chief supported the doctor, "Solid advice, North. I'll get a man to take you downtown."

"I think I'll walk."

"I'll give you a ride," Tiffin tossed in, knowing his offer wouldn't be accepted.

"You get back home to Kaye and the kids." North turned to his boss and put his hand out, "Thank you Chief."

"Don't thank me! I should demote you for disobeying orders!" Then in a quieter tone, "I'm glad you found her and not a minute too soon by the looks of things."

"Bryant got a detail wrong, which might have gotten us to her sooner."

"How's that?"

"He said there were other cabins around, and there weren't. This one stood alone on a private lane."

"Maybe he was mistaken," the Chief said as he lit his pipe and tossed the match toward an ashtray.

"Or, maybe he really wanted to put the screws to us."

"Guess we'll never know."

North crushed the Bradmore onto his head, tossed his jacket over his shoulder and began walking toward the Swanson. At three in the morning, nothing was moving in LaSalle Harbor. There were lights on in a few kitchen windows, and in the distance he could hear the sound of a tug boat, its diesel engines being pushed hard. "A freighter must have come into port," he thought to himself.

He stopped under the yellow glow of a streetlight long enough to light a Pall Mall. He pushed the lighter back into his trouser pocket and put his hand on the butt of the .38 slung under his right arm. He wanted to use it. He wanted to put its barrel in Como's mouth and pull the trigger. As he walked along he pictured the back of the mobster's head explode and the gelatinous contents of his thick Italian skull spread over the wall behind him.

The more he walked, the more the anger welled up in him. The emotions that he'd been packing down suddenly overwhelmed him and, stopping in the dark, his body convulsed and he screamed, "Goddammit, God fucking dammit." The barking of a dog that had been roused out of its sleep brought North back to the moment. He ran his arm across his eyes and worked at repacking his feelings into the dark corners of his mind where he kept them hidden.

Back at his room he pushed his shoes off and swung the leather holster off his back and onto the chair. His shirt was drenched as was the worn brown leather. He cracked the window and pulled the cork from the nearby bottle of bourbon. He took a large sip, followed by another before he stretched out on the mattress. Relief and anger mixed in his mind as he fell into a troubled sleep.

He found himself running along the white sand of a Lake Michigan beach, waves crashed against the shore as a summer squall approached from the West. Mist and sand mixed and pelted his skin. A few hundred yards in front of him was Sylvia who was being held about the waist by Como. He ran until his legs ached and he was gulping air, but he couldn't get any closer to them. "Help me, Brick!" Sylvia cried out, "Help me!"

A crack of thunder woke him. Rain blew in the window and North recognized the thunder and moisture had given his dream its backdrop. He rolled his wrist over and tried to focus on the dial of his watch. It was either eight twenty or four forty. He struggled to get his mind around the problem and realized that it must be after eight. With some effort, he pushed himself up and sat on the side of the bed. He lit a cigarette and drew its smoke deep into his lungs, slowly exhaling through his nostrils. He stood up and splashed some water on his face.

The mirror over the sink revealed the dark bags under his eyes. "You look like shit, North," he said in his best impersonation of Chief Cummings.

After relieving himself in the common bathroom, he decided to get to work on himself. Back in his room, he unfolded his pocketknife and began cutting the bandages off his torso. There was both pain and pleasure having the binding removed. Grabbing his kit, he went back to the bathroom and showered.

He picked up his suit from the chair where he had thrown it the night before, considered otherwise and grabbed the clothes that he had sent to the cleaners. He pushed his legs into the pants and pulled on a clean white shirt. He noticed some discomfort around his torso as he pulled the still damp holster over his shoulders and shoved the .38 into place.

In the lobby he stopped and grabbed a copy of the LaSalle Palladium from the newsstand and tossed a dime on the counter. The youth who sold sundries asked, "Time for a shine?"

North looked at his shoes and nodded. The teen pointed toward the elevated seat with an exaggerated gesture. "I hope you don't mind me saying so, but your shoes are kinda beat."

"Not as beat as I am kid," North said as he scanned through the paper. When his shoes were done he tossed the kid a half dollar.

"Gee, thanks Mr. North!"

At the Fifth Wheel he slammed a cup of coffee and wolfed down a plate of eggs and fried potatoes. He left the paper on the counter. No mention that Sylvia had been found. He decided to see if the Chief would get that detail kept out of the afternoon edition, thinking it might be good to know something his enemies didn't for a change.

He flagged down a cab and rode in silence back to Memorial Hospital. As the cab bounced over the uneven paving bricks of Pipestone Boulevard, the previous night's events ran through his head. "If that goddamn train hadn't been there, we'd gotten to her quicker," he thought to himself, wondering if it would have made a difference.

He climbed the stairs to the lobby which housed a dozen vinyl clad chairs and a couple of small tables with magazines and ashtrays. Directly across from the main doors was a window in the wall, an older woman sat behind a desk which backed up to it.

"May I help you sir?" the matron asked.

"Sylvia Kingston," North said matter-of-factly.

"Miss Kingston is on four south, but she's not to have visitors."

He flashed his badge, "I'm not exactly a visitor."

"You still can't go up there."

"Stop me."

The elevator doors closed just as an orderly ran toward him. He took a moment to slow his breathing as he leaned against the back of the car. The needle over the door leisurely climbed toward his floor number. With a slight bump the car stopped and slowly aligned its doors with the outer pair, which when accomplished, slid open. Doc Howard was waiting on the other side.

"Where is she, Doc?" he demanded.

"She's down the hall, but let's talk first," the doctor looked older, "she's had a rough night."

"What do you mean by that?"

"Her heart stopped about six. We had to give her mouth-to-mouth resuscitation."

"Mouth to what?" North asked incredulously.

"A doctor in Baltimore developed it last year. We push on the victims chest to keep blood flowing and breathe into their mouth to keep oxygen in their lungs."

"I don't need a medical lecture, I need to know that Syl's okay."

"She's breathing on her own, her pulse is still weak, but it gets stronger as we get more fluid into her. This much is certain; she wouldn't have made it until this morning if you hadn't found her."

"Can I talk to her?"

"She's still unconscious, but you can see her for a minute if you'd like." With that Howard led the detective down the tan and taupe tiled corridor. The doctor stopped before he swung a door open, "Be prepared, she looks pretty bad."

The doctor wasn't joking around. Sylvia looked tiny in the hospital bed. Her skin was taught and red, her eyes were sunken and her lips were deeply cracked. Bug bites covered her arms, neck and lower legs. An IV bottle hung on a metal frame, its rubber tube terminated under tape on her upper torso.

"It's okay," Howard said toward as a nurse who had been sitting quietly in a chair next to the bed began to rise, "he won't be staying."

North leaned down and whispered something into Sylvia's ear before he turned to his old friend, "You call me if anything happens."

Doc Howard gave a nod and watched the detective leave the room. The door closed with a solid thud. He looked at the nurse, "And you call me if anything changes."

The switch-board manager caught his eye as he walked into the Safety Building. "How is she?" Midge queried in a soft voice.

North lied, "Doc Howard says she's a tough cookie and will be home soon."

"When you see her, would you tell her that we're all praying for her?"

North rolled the thought around in his head momentarily; in his experience prayer was a waste of energy. "Sure, Midge," he tried to sound sincere, "sure."

Tiffin was hanging up the phone as North entered the squad room, "We going snake hunting?" he asked with a serious note in his voice.

"Oh yeah, snake and wannabe big shot hunting, too."

Tiffin nodded in understanding, "I did a little digging and found that there's a house registered to a Leon Nelson at 422 Tenth. That's two blocks north of Gray. What you want to bet that Sam the Snake is related?"

"Good work, partner." He turned toward the Chief who was leaving his office, "You spare us a couple of uniforms while we go politely ask Mr. Snake to come and visit?"

"Two enough?" Cummings asked.

"I think two will be plenty," he said confidently. He and Tiffin met two officers in the parking lot. "Detective Tiffin and I will come up tenth from Gray, you two come down from Britain. Park a few houses down and we'll walk up to the house together. You two politely knock on the front door, the detective and I will be out back."

The junior of the two officers looked puzzled, "You don't want to knock?"

Tiffin answered, "Trust him, this guy isn't going to wait around to talk to you."

The Mainline coasted to a stop in front of a house about two doors down from the Nelson place. About the same time a marked police car stopped a couple of doors north of the location. North looked toward the officers and raised his left hand palm out and two fingers on his right hand. The officers nodded. He and Tiffin quietly walked behind the house where they were and moved past it until they were encamped next to an outbuilding behind the Nelson house. Through the open windows they heard the doorbell.

Moments later the screen door on the back of the house burst open. Tiffin stepped out from his location and directly in front of Nelson. The large man lowered his shoulder and used Tiffin as a tackling dummy. The two went down in a heap, the detective on the bottom. As Nelson began to push himself up and continue his flight he found himself staring down the barrel of North's Colt.

"Going somewhere, Snake?" North asked sarcastically. Nelson looked like he was contemplating his options. "Don't fool yourself; I have no problem killing you. Shame your grandma will have to hose your blood off her lawn."

Tiffin worked himself back to his feet and began to handcuff Nelson. He had just gotten a cuff tightened around Nelson's right wrist when the drug dealer pulled his left arm free from Tiffin's grasp and swung his elbow into the detective's midsection. Tiffin fell backward as Nelson lounged toward North who, as promised, fired one round. The bullet entered high on Nelson's left thigh and proceeded downward until it encountered his femur five inches above the knee. He collided with the ground, screaming in pain.

Tiffin regained his feet beneath himself and cuffed the now bleeding Nelson.

"You shot me in the leg you fuckin' bastard."

"Bad shot, I was aiming for your balls."

North directed the two uniforms that came running at the sound of gun fire, "Go inside and call for an ambulance."

"Yes, sir!" the younger of the two said almost breathlessly, "I've never seen anyone who's been shot before!"

Nelson looked up at the enthusiastic officer, "You can keep your honky eyeballs to yourself, cracker."

"You should be more polite to him, if you want him to get you an ambulance," North said as he walked toward his partner. "You okay, Tiff?"

"Damn, I'm pretty sure my belly button got pushed into my spine."

"From the grunt you made when he hit you, I think you might be right. Let's get him patched up and see what he's willing to tell us."

It took about fifteen minutes for the ambulance from Kerlikowske Funeral Home to show up. In the meantime the officers and Tiffin searched the house to see what might be hidden inside.

"Nelson's grandmother didn't give us any problem, but we didn't come up with anything. She says that since her husband died, Sammy boy here has been helping her with the bills," Tiffin said as he stepped out the backdoor.

Two men from the funeral home got Nelson onto the gurney and rolled it into the back of the ambulance. North looked at his partner, "Grab the car and meet me at the hospital, I'll ride in the back with my new best friend to make sure he doesn't get any bright ideas."

## Chapter 12

**N**orth pulled his hat off and scratched the top of his head. Nelson, laying on his handcuffed hands and strapped to the gurney, looked up at him, "What you botherin' me for? I ain't done nothin'."

"Oh, but you have, at the very least I've got you selling heroin in violation of the Harrison Act."

"You ain't found no heroin."

"That'll turn up; at the moment, I've got you."

The ambulance bounced over several railroad tracks and Nelson whimpered in pain. "That leg hurting you there Snake?"

"If I weren't tied down, I'd whoop your ass."

North took his thumb and drove it through the bandage and into the entry wound on the bound man's leg. Nelson immediately screamed, the two ambulance men in the front of the car pretended not to notice. "While we're on the way to the hospital, why don't you tell me how you get the smack you're peddling?"

Nelson recovered slightly from the nauseating rush of pain that had overwhelmed him, "You can fuck yourself, I ain't telling you nothin'."

North's thumb found the wound again, this time pushing hard enough that blood began to soak through the bandage. "Mother fucker...," Nelson screamed.

"Now, I'm very politely going to ask you again, how do you get the smack you're selling?"

"I pick it up from a shop out on Territorial Road," Nelson shrieked through gritted teeth.

Relieving the pressure on the wound North looked into Nelson's eyes, "Where on Territorial?"

"Out by the airport."

"What kind of shop?"

"Some tool and die shop, I don't know man."

"Can you show me?"

"Like I can show your honky ass anything, I'm goin' to the hospital."

North knocked on the glass between the back and the men in the front of the car, "Take a detour, drive out Territorial toward the airport. I'm looking for a tool and die company."

The driver nodded and the car made a hard left at the next light and began heading to the airport.

"You can't do that, man," Nelson protested, "you gotta take me to the hospital."

"I do and I will," North said and he took a deep drag on a cigarette, "but at the moment, you're going to point out that shop."

They drove on about five minutes when North tapped on the window, "Slow down and help me look around, I'm looking for a tool and die company, can't be many out here."

Within a couple of minutes the driver said, "Michigan Tool and Die on our left."

North pushed Nelson's head over so he was looking out the window, "Is that it?!"

"Yeah, that's it, that's it! Get me to the hospital man, my fucking leg is going to fall off!"

The ambulance made a couple of turns and they were on Pipestone heading toward the hospital. "Who delivers the drugs to the shop?"

"I don't know, man."

"Who gives you the drugs when you go there?"

"No one, there in a wooden shed on the back of the building."

"And what about the money, where do you leave that?"

"Same place, man."

The detective inhaled deeply through the cigarette and slowly blew the smoke out of his nose while he thought, "How do you know to make a pick up?"

"They call my gram's house and leave a message."

"They call your grandmother and tell her you can pick up the drugs?" North asked doubtfully.

"No, man, they say they have work for me."

North's thumb hovered over the bullet hole, "And when's the last time you had work?"

"Been almost a week, it's about time."

"They come the same time every week?"

144

"Nah, they come when they come."

The ambulance rolled into the emergency entrance. "We're not done talking," North said as the gurney was rolled out of the back of the red and white car.

Tiffin was walking toward his partner as he was exiting the car, "What took you so long? I've been here for almost twenty minutes."

"Snake there showed me where he picks up the drugs."

"Where?"

"A machine shop out by Lakeland."

"Mighty big coincidence," Tiffin said as they walked toward the Mainline.

"I've learned there's no such thing as a coincidence, partner."

"I know, only a connection we haven't put together yet." He tossed the keys over the car and into North's open hand.

North turned the ignition key and pressed the starter, "It's time we start making that connection." The car lurched onto the road and back toward Michigan Tool and Die.

Tiffin rolled a cigarette thoughtfully between his thumb and index finger as the car passed block after block of row houses, "So, what's the plan?"

"The only plan I have is to see who at the machine shop is involved and convince them to talk."

Row houses gave way to stately homes on large lots and finally passed to parks and churches before they were downtown and making their way onto Territorial and back toward the airport.

It was a little after one when they pulled onto the oil covered dirt parking lot of the machine shop. The sound of heavy machinery came from an open door and sweat, which had begun its journey on North's head, rolled down between his shoulder blades. He left his jacket and hat in the car.

Tiffin walked into the office door just in front of his partner. A large floor fan droned in the corner pushing a ridiculous amount of air through the small vacant room. "Anyone here?" Tiffin shouted over the noise of the fan and equipment running on the shop floor.

Nudging him, North pointed toward the large shop where a half dozen men were milling parts at various machines. One of the men saw them and turned the machine he was using off, which made no difference in the level of noise in the building. As he walked toward the detectives he tapped another worker on the shoulder and used his head to point to their guests. That man grabbed a large wrench, left his machine and walked toward where North and Tiffin were standing.

"What can we do for you?" the first man asked.

Over the din North bellowed, "We have a couple of questions, mind if we step outside to talk about them?"

He nodded and, trailed by his coworker with the wrench, followed the detectives through the office and outside.

"What's this about?" the vocal of the two men asked.

"We're working vice," Tiffin lied, "and got word that an illegal poker game is being held here." He look between the men and then to North.

"That's right," his partner agreed.

"That's bullshit!" the man with the wrench offered, "If we had time to play cards we wouldn't be working on a Saturday, would we?"

Tiffin eyed the leader, "So you won't mind us taking a little look around?"

"Do whatever the fuck you want. Look around and get lost."

The detectives nodded and the two laborers went back to their respective machines. North wiped his brow with his handkerchief, "Good job, partner. You're becoming a regular liar. Let's check out the shop space so we look legit before we find that shed Snake told us about."

They walked through the building, spending little time in the office, on the machine floor and a warehouse area before walking into a lunch room which was home to a metal table and chairs, a small row of metal lockers and a toilet and sink against the wall.

"Nice!" North whistled. "Have your sandwich, take a shit and talk to your pals all at the same time." As he spoke he quickly looked through the lockers. In the last he found a work shirt with the name Butch embroidered on it. "Hey Tiff, take a look at this."

Tiffin looked the shirt over, "There's got to be a lot of guys with the nickname of Butch."

"Can't be a coincidence," he said as he put the shirt back into the locker. "Let's check out that shed."

More of a lean-to, the wooden shed backed up to the rear of the building. The top was hinged and North lifted it to reveal four fifty-five gallon drums, each labeled Machine Oil. With the exception of the one in the right rear corner, each was sealed with a metal band that held the lid firmly in place. North leaned over and carefully lifted the lid, "Nice and clean in there, and there's a wooden crate inside that takes up most of the space."

"Like a table to put things on?" Tiffin inquired.

"Exactly what I was thinking. Let's get out of here before anyone inside catches on."

North slid behind the wheel, "What say we check if that brunette at Lakeland can tell us anything about Butch."

"Suzette," Tiffin offered.

"How's that?"

"Suzette, the name of the brunette at the airport."

"Uh huh," North absentminded replied, his thoughts on Syl.

He managed to park in the shade outside the terminal building. Both detectives slid their coats and hats on as they walked into the lobby.

"Detective North!," Suzette offered breathily, "you aren't going to make me talk to your married partner again, are you?"

North pulled his notepad and pencil from his pocket, "No doll, this time I want to talk to you."

"What do you need to know?" Then eyeing Tiffin, she lowered her voice, "Maybe you want to see me in private."

"Some other time, perhaps." He fingered through his notepad and found his notes from Monday morning, "Butch Henry, what can you tell me about him?"

"Butch? I don't know, quiet."

"I'm not looking for a one word answer, doll. What can you tell me about him?"

"Oh, he's married, got half a dozen kids, been here longer than I have. Keeps to himself. That kind of thing?"

"Anything different about him now, than when you first met him?"

"Like what?"

"I don't know. Is he more tense, less tense, happier, grumpier? That kind of thing."

"Well, he seems to be a lot happier nowadays. He got a new station wagon that he keeps wiping the dust off of when he passes it."

Tiffin looked up from the notes he was taking, "Is his car here now?"

Suzette pointed through the window and across the tarmac, "Sure, it's the red and white one by hanger two."

"One more question doll," North brought her attention back to himself, "Does Butch work anywhere other than here?"

"You mean does he moonlight?"

"Yeah, that's what I mean."

"Sure, I've heard him talk about working at some factory near here. Why?"

"Just curious," North closed his notepad. "Thanks doll."

Putting a pout on her lips, "You ever going to call me?" she asked as the detectives walked away from the counter.

North turned and looked over his shoulder. He took a hard look that started at her legs, which she crossed as she sat down, past her ample breasts and into her eyes, "Not today, doll. Not today." With that he pushed the door open and walked back into the July afternoon.

As they were driving to Butch's car, they saw him climb in and drive off toward the main road. North punched the gas and within moments were on his bumper. Tiffin shone the red light and sounded the siren. Butch made a hard right hand turn down a dirt service road and pulled through the open doors of an outbuilding. North stopped the car just outside the door that Butch had pulled into. At the sound of their car doors shutting, the maintenance man looked out from the shadows of the building. "Mr. Henry," Tiffin shouted, "we need to talk with you."

Butch turned and ran into the dimness of the building. "Dammit, Tiff, don't announce us like that, they always run when we announce ourselves."

The two ran from the bright sunlight into the darkness of the building, their eyes struggled to see. North felt the rush of air as a two-by-four raced past his head and landed with a thud on the back of Tiffin's neck. Tiffin collided face first with the concrete.

North spun and managed to grab the piece of lumber with his right hand as it hurtled toward his head. Using the momentum of the swing, he pulled Butch slightly off his feet and brought his left fist into firm contact with the maintenance worker's jaw. He wasn't quite sure if the crack was his knuckles or Butch's face. But it hardly matter as Butch was splayed on the floor next to Tiffin.

"Barry!" North barked over the sound of a small plane which had just taken off, "You okay?"

Tiffin slowly lifted an arm and put his hand on the back of his neck, "Did you just call me by my first name?" I don't think you've ever called me by my first name."

"Hell, I thought you were dead and was practicing using it for your eulogy. Think you can walk?"

"Sure. What about Butch?"

North flexed his fingers on his left hand, "From the sound of it, I might have broken his jaw."

Slow to get his feet under himself, Tiffin sat on his haunches for a moment. North reached out and offered his partner a hand, "Let's get Butch here downtown and see what he's got to say for himself."

In the corner of the building was a bucket filled with stagnant water. North grabbed the bucket and tossed the contents onto the prostrate maintenance man. "Time to wake up sunshine."

Butch looked startled, as if trying to remember why he was on the floor and why he was wet. It took him only a moment to come to his senses, "What do you want?"

151

"Let's start with why you tried to kill me," Tiffin said as he rubbed his neck.

"I wasn't trying to kill you, I haven't done anything."

North looked over the man on the floor, "And every innocent man tries to take the head off a detective. Why'd you run?"

"Guess 'cuz I wanted to get away from you."

"Yeah, kind of thought that was the case. Tell me why?"

"I don't know, I just figured you were going to arrest me."

"Well, if we weren't before, we are now."

They handcuffed him and slid him into the back of the Mainline. Tiffin sat in the backseat while North took the wheel. Rubbing his neck, he shouted up to the front seat, "I'm going to need some aspirin when we get to the office."

# Chapter 13

T he windowless interview room was stifling. A bead of sweat rolled down Butch Henry's nose and dangled from the tip for a moment before it plopped onto the table behind which he was seated. North took a slow sip from a glass of ice water and centered it in a ring of condensation as he put it down.

"I sure am thirsty," Butch said, and then mostly to himself, "and my jaw hurts."

North looked up from the glass, "Do you always bitch this much, Butch?"

"I'm just saying I'm thirsty, that's all."

"Maybe if you tell me what I need to know, I can find you a glass of water."

"I don't know anything."

"You work at Michigan Tool and Die, do you?"

"Sometimes, when they need help, mostly I just sweep up."

"You ever take things there?"

Henry squirmed slightly in his chair, "I don't know what you're talking about."

"Sure you do. You take a package, put it in a barrel in the shed behind the building and make a phone call, isn't that right?"

Startled that the detective knew so much, Butch looked around nervously, "Okay, sure, but that isn't against the laws."

153

North's tone turned dark, "What's in the package, Bill?"

"I don't know, I just put the package in the drum and call a number I was given."

"And later you go back and pick up another package, isn't that right?"

Butch dropped his head, "Yeah, I do that too."

"Where do you get the package?"

Butch looked down at his hands which were handcuffed to a ring on the table. North slammed the palm of his hand on the tabletop causing the maintenance worker to jump. "Where do you get the package?"

"I can't tell you, he'll kill me," he said in a trembling voice.

North looked into his eyes, "There are four reasons to kill someone, money, love, anger and fear; I think we can rule out love, that leaves us money, anger and fear. So, Butch, which is it? Why would someone want to kill you?"

"Anger," he said in a whisper.

"What?"

"He'll kill me because he'll be mad at me."

"Who will kill you Bill?"

Tears began rolling down his cheeks, "I can't tell you."

"That's not true, Bill. You can and you will tell me."

"Please, I've got a wife and kids, I can't tell you."

North stood, picked up the glass of water and turned toward the door, "Maybe you'll want to talk later." He pulled the door open and slammed it behind himself. He could hear crying in the room behind him.

Tiffin was seated at his desk; he held an icepack against his neck, "How'd it go?"

"Well, he admits that he carries packages to the machine shop and packages back to someone."

"Who?"

"He's having some trouble telling me, I'm giving him some time to think about it."

Tiffin repositioned the icepack on his neck, "Can't be a coincidence that he's the one that found Michelle Denslow's body."

"Not true. He may have found it like he said he did. I don't think he'd have called the police if he'd been involved with dropping her there in the first place."

"Maybe he called because he wanted to take suspicion off himself."

"No, the guy I just interviewed doesn't seem to have that kind of constitution. We'll find out more when we go back in to talk to him."

"When do you want to go back in?"

"Oh, an hour of sweating should be about enough," North swallowed his remaining water and held the glass up to the late afternoon light coming in the window. He thought about how hot it was in the interrogation room and how thirsty their prisoner said he was. For a moment he pictured Sylvia in stifling heat with no water. "Dammit," he said as he filled a glass from the cooler in the corner, "let's go in now."

Tiffin and he quietly entered the interrogation room and North put the glass of water down in front of Butch who eagerly raised it to his lips.

North stood over their prisoner, "Look Butch, I eyeball you and I see a decent guy who's gotten himself in some deep water. I can be a life preserver, but you need to tell me what I need to know."

Tiffin sat down on the opposite side of the table. "Here's the skinny, you've got yourself mixed up with the sale of narcotics and possibly two murders. We don't want you to go down for something you haven't done. Tell us what you know and we won't prosecute you for what you didn't do."

The panicked look returned to Butch's face, "I don't know anything about narcotics, and I haven't killed anybody. I'm sorry I hit you, can I please just go home?"

North bent down to his ear and said very quietly, "Tell me who you get the package from and who you take the cash back to." Butch looked down and shook his head.

Tiffin took a very friendly tone, "Here's how this works. You help us, we take the bad guy off the street and maybe I'll even forget you tried to take my head off."

Butch looked between the two detectives, "Okay, but you gotta make sure he doesn't hurt me."

"Who Butch?" North asked, "So who doesn't hurt you?"

"Jaeger," the name came out almost like a sob, "Mr. Jaeger gives me the packages and I hide them at the tool and die shop."

North stood up, "And you give the money to Mr. Jaeger also?"

"I give him a small box, I don't know what's inside it."

"Not the curious type, Butch?"

"It's none of my business."

Tiffin looked up from the notes he was taking, "Does Jaeger pay you to do this job for him?"

"I get ten, sometimes twenty for doing it."

"And how often do you make these deliveries?"

"Sometimes once or twice a week," Butch said nervously.

North gave a little whistle, "You're picking up eighty to a hundred dollars a month and you didn't think there was anything hinky about that?"

"I bring home sixty-four dollars a week from the airport. That doesn't go too far. That's why I started to moonlight at the tool and die. I can pick up another fifteen when they need me. So no, I wasn't going to look a gift horse in the mouth."

"Bill, I'm going to get an officer who will to take you down to the holding cells and process you."

"Oh please, don't put me in a jail cell."

"Think of it as keeping you safe."

"I need to call my wife."

"The officer will see that you can call her," North paused for a moment, "is there somewhere your wife and kids can go?"

"I guess, why?"

"Have her gather your kids and get somewhere, I don't want Jaeger looking for you and catching them off guard."

Butch looked at the floor demurely, "Thank you, sir."

A uniformed officer led Butch out of the squad room and toward the elevator that would take him to the cells. The detectives sat at their desks, North was obviously deep in thought.

Tiffin broke the silence, "Mind sharing your thoughts?"

"As far as we know, Jaeger doesn't know we have Butch. His car is in an abandoned building, we've got to get him with evidence, we've got to get him to confess, or we've got nothing on him."

"And Nelson and Henry will go free because we've really got nothing on them."

"And that's a problem. Nelson points to Henry, Henry points to Jaeger and we need Jaeger to point us to Como."

"Daisy chain with each one screwing the other, huh?" Tiffin observed as he looked at his partner.

"Cluster fuck if we can't get Jaeger to turn on Como."

"So, how are we going to do that?"

North looked up at the clock, "We've got a little bit of time to think this through. Why don't you get home to Kaye, I'm going to check in on Syl."

North grabbed his coat and hat along with the keys to the Mainline. As he passed the dispatch office, Midge called out, "Hey Brick, if you're going to see Sylvia, the girls chipped in for some flowers, would you mind taking them to her?"

Not knowing what else to say, he nodded, "Yeah, sure. I can do that."

She turned into the office and brought out a small vase with a bouquet of bright blooms. Midge smiled, "Here's a card that goes with them; we all signed it."

He juggled the vase, card, his hat and the car keys, "I'll get these to her."

"Goodnight detective, thank you."

His urge was to drop the flowers into the nearest trash bin, but he caught himself. He rolled down the windows, opened the vent in the Ford and smoked a cigarette while he waited for the car to cool down a bit. Once he thought it would be tolerable, he climbed in and headed toward the hospital. He was pleased to be able to park in the shadow the building cast. With flowers in hand, he rode the elevator to the fourth floor.

A nurse caught his attention as he passed, "Are you here to see Miss Kingston?"

"Yea, that's right."

"Doctor Howard asked to see you before you see her."

"Tell Doc Howard," he started to say something in an angry tone and stopped himself, "tell Doc Howard that I'm here."

She picked up a telephone and dialed three digits. North watched as her finger spun the dial, one-four-seven. With each sweep he could hear the clicking of the dial as it returned to the rest position. "Doctor Howard? Yes, this is Nurse Fisher up on four. The man you wanted to see is here." She nodded as the doctor spoke to her, "He says have a seat, he'll be up in just a couple of minutes."

North was uncomfortable taking directions in the best of times and this time was no different. He sat down and watched the needle over the elevator. It stayed at the first floor for quite a while before it moved to the basement level, and finally its slow journey to the top floor. He stood up as the doors slid to the side.

Doc Howard tried to make a happy face toward North, but it wasn't forthcoming, "Why don't we have a chat for a minute?"

"What's going on, Doc?"

"There's something you should know," he paused to find the right words, "Sylvia is beginning to show signs of brain damage."

"What do you mean signs?"

"To use medical jargon, she's beginning to posture," he made fists and pulled them up toward his face while dropping his chin to his chest, not unlike a boxer protecting face from an opponent's buffets. "It's a classic sign of brain damage."

North's mind reeled, "What are you telling me?"

"I'm telling you that I don't know if she's going to live and if she does, I don't know that she'll be who she was."

The detective just stood there for a moment staring at his friend, "Son of a bitch, Doc. Son of a bitch."

"Brick, I warned you when you brought her in that her temperature was dangerously high."

"Isn't there anything you can do for her?"

"We're giving her fluids and her kidneys are beginning to work. We're making her comfortable and we'll keep monitoring her. Time, Brick, we just have to wait."

North nodded to Doc Howard and turned to the nurse, "See that these flowers and card get into her room." He walked over to the elevator and pushed the button. The car arrived and he stepped in. He didn't turn around until the doors had shut.

Once outside he leaned against the fender of the car and smoked a cigarette. He tried to make sense out of the information he'd just been given, but his mind refused to accept it. He got into the car and began an aimless drive which took him first to the docks where he watched a freighter offloading Portland cement. He then drove up the coast for a few miles and watched the sun dip into Lake Michigan. Instead of taking the car back to the motor pool, he drove to the Sheffield and went up to Sylvia's apartment.

He reached over the door and found the key on ledge of the transom window. He inserted it into the lock and stepped into the room. Everything was as he had left it, the sofa cushions in front of the easy chair, the bed pulled out with Sylvia's nightclothes where she had tossed them. He picked up the kimono robe and held it to his nose for a moment. Memories of their last night together washed over him. He recalled with uneasiness that his last interaction with her had been to slip out from under her because he was uncomfortable.

He folded the robe, boxers and top she had last worn and put them on the coffee table. He grabbed the pillows from the bed, tossed them into the closet and folded the mattress in on itself. Cushions finally in place, he checked the little refrigerator hoping to find a beer before he remembered that they had split the last one she had.

If he was honest he would have to admit that in the dozen visits he had made to this apartment, he had paid more attention to the occupant than to the room itself. He switched on the lamp and looked at two photographs which hung on the wall. One was of Sylvia as a teen with an Irish Setter and a blue ribbon. The ribbon itself was pinned to the wall next to the photo, "Wayne County Kennel Club, Junior Best of Show 1949" it boasted. The other was of Sylvia and two older adults. "Parents?" he thought to himself. On the small shelf under the coffee table was an autograph album. He leafed through it and found that it was mostly notes from high school friends, "Dear Syl," one said, "I wish you all the best in the future. You're one cool kittie! Love, Denise." The others were like it with the exception of autographs from Doris Day and Henry Fonda, both of which had "Fox Theatre 1953" written under them in Sylvia's hand.

He carefully replaced the album and looked out the window to the street below. A few cars passed by, but otherwise the streets were empty. He took one last look at the room, turned off the light and locked the door behind himself.

After dropping the Ford back at the Safety Building he popped into the Fifth Wheel, "Got anything left?" he asked as he walked into the nearly empty café.

"Get you some chicken and dumplings if you want," came the response from the counter.

After a quick supper he walked back to the Swanson and up to his room. He pulled the cork from the bottle of Old Quaker and poured the remaining few ounces into a glass. Stripped of his clothes he propped himself up on the bed and sipped the bourbon while he tried to put things together in his mind.

"Did Jaeger know Denslow's body was in the hanger? Maybe, maybe not. Did Jaeger know the plane belonged to Dalander? He must have. Why did he offer up Dalander's name as the registered owner? He knew we might contact Civil Aviation to verify. Was Dalander bringing drugs in from Como? Probably. Was Dalander selling the drugs to Jaeger? Without doubt. Has he been doing it for a while? Probably not, if he had money Jaeger would still be screwing the Williams woman."

He mulled over thoughts for some time before he swallowed the last of the bourbon. Suddenly, he jumped out of bed and pulled on his shirt, pants and shoes and leafed through his notepad. He strapped on his holster, spun the cylinder of the Colt, clicked it shut and shoved it under his arm. He pushed his arms into his jacket and slammed the door as he raced to the payphone in the lobby. He dropped a dime into the phone and glanced at his notes as he dialed Yukon 5-2215.

The number was answered with a breathy "Hello?"

"Suzette, it's Detective North."

163

"Brick! You said you weren't going to call."

"I need to talk to you, is there somewhere we can meet?"

"Why don't you come up to my place?"

"Are you alone?"

"Not once you get here."

"Look doll, I've got some police business I need to speak with you about."

"Oh, if that's how you want to play it, I'm game."

"Just tell me where you live; I'll explain when I get there."

"Six twenty-five Colfax, second floor on the left."

"Be there in fifteen minutes," North said as he hung up the phone. Colfax Avenue was about two miles away and he thought about hailing a cab. Instead he walked the five minutes back to the Safety Building and grabbed the Mainline. By his reckoning, he arrived at the Colfax address within the time frame he had allotted himself.

The large older home Suzette lived in had been divided into apartments during the war. Suzette's apartment was easy to locate and the door opened immediately at his knock. He stepped into the dimly lit room and the door closed behind him. He turned to see that the door had blocked his view of the brunette who stood before him in a sheer white teddy which revealed not only her pendulous breasts but all of her other assets as well.

"Is this where you handcuff me and make me confess?" she said in a sultry voice.

"I'm really here to discuss a case."

She stepped behind him, reached around and began to loosen the buttons on his shirt, "Oh, I'm sure you are. I think you'll find that you'll need to pump me for information before you make me squeal."

North turn around, put his hands on her shoulders and gently moved her back, "I really do need to talk to you about police business." There was a lump in his throat as he looked at her; she really was a very beautiful woman.

"You're serious?"

"I'm afraid so, doll."

She walked out of the living room and came back with a light weight robe which she slipped on.

"What's so important that you need to see me tonight?"

He told her what he knew about her boss and outlined the plan he had come up with, "You think you can do that?"

She sat down on the sofa, "For you, I'd do anything. When do you want me to do it?"

"Tomorrow."

"Okay, I can do that. Sure you don't want to stay," she said in a voice that could melt steel.

"I better get back. I have the feeling that tomorrow is going to be a long day."

She leaned back on the sofa and, like a Radio City Rockette doing the Christmas show, brought one exquisite leg high up before seductively crossing it over the other, "You just might be missing the best night of your life."

He paused to look at her for a moment before he turned and left. As he walked out of the apartment he heard what sounded like a slipper hit the door as he made his way down the stairs.

## Chapter 14

**B**ack at the Swanson, North took a hot shower and returned to his room to shave. He lay on the bed and hoped to catch a little breeze through the open window. Neither the breeze nor sleep were forthcoming.

He tossed and turned as thoughts of Sylvia, Butch, Jaeger and Suzette raced through his mind. Around five he rose, gathered his belongings and made a call from the lobby.

"Hello?"

"Meet me at the Howard Johnson's out on M-139 as soon as you can."

"Brick?" Tiffin's tone was incredulous, "what time is it?"

"About a quarter after five. I've got an idea."

"Crap, can't it wait until the sun comes up?"

"No, I'll see you there," North hung up the phone.

"Fine, but you're buying," Tiffin said into the dead line.

As Tiffin pulled into the parking lot he spotted the Mainline parked near the front door. He entered and looked around the nearly empty restaurant; he finally spotted North in a corner booth, his back to the wall.

North looked up from his coffee cup, "Took you long enough."

"Yeah well, I had to do a few things, like shave and get dressed. What's so blasted important that we're meeting at this hour?"

167

A waitress wandered over with as little enthusiasm as one can muster at the end of an overnight shift, "Coffee?"

Tiffin nodded as she put a cup down and poured coffee from the carafe that was already on the table, "You want anything else?"

"Yeah, drop an order of flapjacks, a couple of eggs over easy and sausage."

The waitress nodded and walked away. North took another swig of coffee as he waited for her to get out of earshot, "I came up with a plan to get Jaeger and Como."

"Do tell."

"As far as we know, Jaeger doesn't know we have Nelson or Henry. So as far as he's concerned it's business as usual."

"Until Butch doesn't show up to work this morning."

"I've got that covered."

"How's that?"

"He's going to call in sick."

"And how's he going to do that?"

"Let's say I've got someone on the inside who's going to help."

A light came on behind Tiffin's eyes, "Suzette!"

"Suzette," North repeated.

The waitress brought the order and put it in front of Tiffin along with the check which he pushed over to his partner, "Thank you," he said to the waitress and then repeated it to North.

Tiffin pushed a fork full of food into his mouth, "And then what?"

North began to outline his plan as Tiffin ate.

He heard him out while he finished the plate, "What if Jaeger doesn't bite?"

"If he's as hungry as I think he is, he won't be able to resist the bait."

Tiffin smiled as North paid the tab at the counter. He followed the Mainline to the Safety Building and pulled into the lot. He caught sight of North on the stairs as he raced up to the squad room behind him, "I don't think our Mr. Snake is going to be very cooperative."

"I've got that covered. It doesn't have to be Nelson, just someone Jaeger believes is Nelson."

"What about the call to Nelson's grandmother? How's that going to work?"

"Okay, there's a couple of details I haven't worked out. First things first."

As the sun rose they began to flesh out some of the more nebulous details. North went down to the locker room and found the dayshift sergeant putting on his uniform, "Hey Ben."

Ben Higdon and North had been rookies together, "Oh hey Brick, what brings you down to the slums? Missing your uniform days?"

"I miss a regular schedule, that's for sure. Is Officer Davis on today?"

"Sure, he's in by seven forty-five like clockwork. Something wrong?"

"Nah, I just need to see if I can persuade him to do a little job for me."

"Okay with me," Higdon answered as he turned toward the squeaking locker room door. "Here he is now. Davis," he called to the young officer, "Detective North wants a word with you."

Officer Davis was in his early twenties; tall, thin and impeccably groomed. He was also colored.

"Good morning, Davis," North said.

"Good morning, sir," Davis said as he moved into a parade rest position with his hands behind his back.

"Relax, I just need you to do a job for me about 9:30 this morning. Won't take you but a minute."

"If I may ask, what kind of job sir?"

"Just come up to the Detective Squad Room at 9:30, I'll explain then and have you on your beat right after that." He nodded to Higdon who returned the nod. North turned toward the exit as Higdon addressed the officer, "What are you standing there for? Get into uniform and get your ass to the briefing room!"

"Sir, yes sir," came the clipped answer as the door shut behind the detective.

170

Back upstairs Tiffin was just hanging up the phone, "Okay, Ma Bell will redirect calls to the Nelson to our office here. But that means…"

North jumped in, "that means anyone who calls the Nelson's is going to end up talking to us. I hope Mrs. Nelson isn't the kind of woman who gets a lot of calls. When can they get this ready?"

"They have to do something at the telephone exchange down in the Flats. Probably be ready by early this afternoon."

"Okay, that'll work. What'll happen if Mrs. Nelson tries to make a call?"

"Her phone will be dead, she won't get a dial tone."

"Alright, we've got plenty of work to do, let's get to it."

"Mr. Jaeger," Suzette called out as the airport manager rushed into the terminal building carrying his signature lunch bag.

"What is it?" He answered briskly.

"Butch Henry called, he won't be in for a few days."

"Why the hell not?!" Jaeger sputtered as he turned to face her.

"He said that his mother is really ill up in Traverse City and he's on his way up there."

"When's he coming back?"

Suzette straightened herself to full height which was several inches taller than Jaeger even without the heels she was wearing, "He said he'd be gone a few days."

Jaeger, realizing he wasn't going to be able to intimidate the intimidating brunette at the ticket counter, turned and muttered, "Fine."

She waited until he was out of the lobby and well down his office corridor before she made a quick phone call, "He bought it," she said before hanging up.

The detectives filled Cummings in on the plan, "There's a bunch that can go wrong," the Chief said as he took a careful look at them, "but it isn't bad. Go ahead and run with it. Just make sure we have enough to make charges stick in court."

About the time they were walking out of the Chief's office, Davis was walking into the room. North checked the clock, it was exactly nine-thirty, "Punctuality your thing, Davis?" he asked.

"Yes sir. What do you need me to do?"

"You have any acting ability?"

"Uh," the young officer looked surprised, "what do you mean, sir?"

"Do you think you can sound like a thug from the Flats?" Tiffin asked.

"I suppose. What do you need me to say?"

North turned and grabbed a piece of paper from his desk, "Something like this," he said as he handed the paper to Davis. "You may have to make it sound rougher, if you know what I mean? Run through it for me."

The officer read the lines silently to himself, nodded and then read them aloud to North who said, "can you make your voice a little deeper and add a hint of anger to the words."

Davis rehearsed the lines a couple more times before North decided that it was a good approximation.

North looked around the room; Cummings, another detective and a couple of uniforms had gathered, he called down to the dispatch office, "Midge, it's Detective North, I don't want a phone to ring on the second floor until I call you back."

Slightly surprised, she assured him that no calls would be sent upstairs. At that he pressed an outside line button on the phone, dialed and handed the phone to Davis who held the headset away from his ear enough the others could hear.

"Lakeland Airport, how may I help you?" a breathy voice answered.

"Need me to speak to Jaeger."

"One moment, please," came the reply followed by ringing and then, "Airport Manager."

"Jaeger, I got me some hurtin' customers down here. Need you to get me some shit now!" There was a long enough pause that those listening in wondered if he had bought Davis' impersonation.

"What the hell? You can't call me here! You wait until someone calls you!" Jaeger said in a panicked and slightly whispered voice.

Davis looked at the script and improvised, "Can't be waitin' for your honky-ass to be callin'. I got enough business to move a quarter brick of the stuff. If you can't get it for me, I'll find someone else who can supply. You see what I'm sayin'?"

"I'll see what I can do. But you don't call here again!" Jaeger slammed the phone down hard enough that those listening in could hear the bell in the base ring.

Davis hung up the phone and let out a heavy sigh, "How'd I do?"

North slapped him on the back, "I think Nelson's grandmother would have bought it! Good job Davis."

Chief Cummings offered a hand which the young officer took, "Do good work, keep your nose clean and maybe someday you'll find yourself up here."

"I'm not sure anyone is ready for a detective that looks like me, sir," Davis replied as he shook the chief's hand.

"I don't care what people look like, I like results. Now, get yourself to your beat."

"Sir, yes sir!" Davis snapped.

"Good kid," Cummings remarked as he turned toward his office, then to North and Tiffin, "I don't want you to fart without telling me, you got me?"

"Got you," Tiffin answered.

Cummings gave North a cold look, "What about you?"

North nodded, "Yeah, I got you."

Jaeger smoked another in a string of cigarettes as he paced his office. He didn't want to call Chicago, he also didn't want to lose a valuable pusher for the boss. "Fucking shit," he said to himself as he picked up the phone. He pressed the button for an outside line and dialed zero.

A nasally female voice answered immediately, "Operator."

"Get me Chicago."

"One moment please." There was a series of clicks as the line was transferred, "Operator," a nearly identical voice said.

"I need Skokie, Fairfax 9-9675."

It seemed like an eternity before the Operator returned. "Hold please… it's ringing now."

A familiar voice answered on the third ring, "Como residence."

Jaeger heart raced, "Connie?"

"Who's this?" she said in an aloof manner.

The racing of his heart dropped a bit and a lump formed in his throat at the thought that she didn't recognize his voice, "It's me, Harold. Harold Jaeger."

"What do you want?"

"I need to speak with Mr. Como."

"Why does he need to speak with you?"

"Look, you got me into this drug business…"

175

"All I did was call and ask if you wanted to make some extra money. You willingly took an offer, that's not on me."

"I thought I could get you back."

"Get me back? That's a laugh. You've got nothing I need. I'm living a life you could never offer. I'll tell him you want to talk to him. He'll call you if and when he wants to." With that the line went dead. Jaeger stood in his office, sweat dripping off his balding head and saturating the collars of both his shirt and suit jacket. He plopped into his chair and lit another cigarette even though one was already burning. A tear rolled down his cheek as he leaned back in the chair and stared at the ceiling.

North and Tiffin walked into the air-conditioned comfort of the Trophy Room. "Roxy, a beer and a bump," North called out as he entered, "and a beer for Tiff here."

The waitress smiled, "You boys look beat."

Tiffin spoke up, "My partner here decided I needed to wake up at five this morning."

The big old gal laughed, "You ought to run a bar, I got upstairs to bed at two-thirty and was back down here at nine."

"No sympathy around here, partner," North said as he threw his coat and hat on the chair next to him. "Maybe Kaye will give you some when you get home."

"Kaye will give me something, but it won't be sympathy. You woke her and the kids too, so she'll be mad at me."

"Yet another reason I'm not married."

Two beers and a shot of whiskey were placed on the table. "You boys eating today?" she said as she wiped up the table next to theirs.

"Let's drink first and we'll let you know," North said without consulting Tiffin.

"Thanks for speaking for me."

"You just ate breakfast; I didn't think you'd want anything else."

"Brick, that was six and a half hours ago." Tiffin got a burger and an order of deep-fried bell pepper rings. North watched him eat and discussed next steps.

"What do you suppose Jaeger is up to?" Tiffin asked as he slid the last bit of burger into his mouth.

North laughed, "Shitting bricks if I had to take a guess."

The phone rang in the airport manager's office; Jaeger answered before the first ring died, "Harold Jaeger."

"What'da ya mean calling and demanding to talk wit me?"

"Mr. Como, I didn't demand anything…"

"And yet, here I am having to pick up the phone and call you. You know what? I should put a bullet up your ass."

"Mr. Como, sir, I've got a dealer here in town who hasn't had a shipment recently, he says he can peddle a quarter brick if I can get it to him."

"A quarter of a brick, are you fuckin' kiddin' me? What kind of collateral you got for me to spot some street dealer with a quarter brick?"

"He's always come through. There hasn't been anything hinky in our dealings together. You have my word."

"Your word?! What the fuck good is your word? You got kids Jaeger?"

"I have two boys, why?"

"'Cuz they just became your collateral, that's why."

"What?" Jaeger was sweating even more than normal, his handkerchief was wet from wiping his brow, "Mr. Como, you don't have to threaten my boys."

"How long we been doin' business, Harold?"

"Six months maybe."

"And in all that time, did you ever think that I make, what do you call 'em, idle threats?"

"No sir, never."

"Good, now you understand. Here's how we're gonna work this. I'm gonna get you a quarter brick; you're gonna guarantee that I'm gonna get my money from it and I decide what it's worth, capeesh?"

"Yes sir, I understand."

"I hope you do. I'll have it on a plane tonight. Just remember this, it's on your ass." The phone went dead and Jaeger sat in his sweat and shook.

Back in the squad room, North left a message for Doc Howard to call. The phone rang about five minutes later, "How's Sylvia, Doc?"

"I saw her not ten minutes ago. Her kidneys are beginning to function well and her heart rate is normal. I'm happy with that."

"Has she come to? How about the brain damage?"

"She has good pupillary response, which is positive, but no, she hasn't awakened."

North ran the information through his mind for a moment, "So her eyes are working, doesn't that mean that her brain is working?"

"Brick, the brain is like what Churchill said about Russia, 'It's a riddle, wrapped in a mystery, inside an enigma.' All we can do is wait."

"Thanks, Doc. Let me know if," he corrected himself, "when she wakes up."

"I will, Brick, I will."

Tiffin hung up his phone about the same time North ended his call, "That was Michigan Bell, they've made the necessary adjustments, calls to the Nelson house will ring directly to your phone." North heard the words, but his mind was five miles away on the fourth floor of the hospital.

"Let's go talk to Butch," North said as he rose from his desk, "I've got a couple more questions for him." They made their way to the cells

179

and had the maintenance man brought to the small interrogation room on the basement level.

Butch seemed pleased to see the detectives as he was led into the room, "Am I free to go?" the words more a plea than a question.

North shook his head, "Part of the reason you're here is for your safety. You've been playing way out of your league."

"I just pick up packages and deliver them, that's all I do."

"And give detectives bruises on their back and neck," Tiffin added.

"I'm real sorry about that, I really am."

North looked at Tiffin then directly into Butch's eye, "How long after you drop the package off at the tool and die does the money come back to you?"

"Usually pretty quick, like a day, sometimes two. Why?"

"Don't worry about the why. How does Jaeger know that it's time for you to pick up the money?"

"I don't know. All I know is that he sends me and I get it."

"Lou," North shouted, and when the older officer opened the door, "Take Mr. Henry back to his cell." North waited to speak until he heard the door of the cell block slam shut, "We're fucked."

Tiffin looked with surprise at his partner, "How's that?"

"Because we don't know how Jaeger is told the money is waiting for him."

"Wouldn't ol' Snake just call him and let him know?"

"Maybe, but what if there's some other way? If we get this wrong, Jaeger might not fall for it."

On their way to the second floor, they found Sergeant Higdon at the desk as they walked through the lobby, "Hey Ben," North called out, "what's the chance of me maybe using Davis for a few days."

"I suppose I could rearrange duty schedules, why?"

"I need him to sit on the phone."

Higdon gave the detectives a quizzical look, "Should I even ask?"

"I'll tell you when everything is done."

The Sergeant nodded and went back to his paperwork. The phone was ringing on North's desk as they entered the squad room; he picked up the phone, "Hello. No, this is Michigan Bell repair. What number are you calling? Sorry, that line is out of order."

Tiffin looked at North with a mixture of surprise and admiration, "How do you do that?"

"Do what?"

"Lie so effortlessly. I'm thinking about what I'm going to say and you're into a full conversation."

"I don't think about it as lying; I prefer to think of it as being able to think on my feet."

"What was the call about?"

"Didn't bother to ask. The important thing is it wasn't Jaeger."

"So, you're going to have Davis just sit here waiting for the phone to ring?"

"Unless you have a better plan, that's it."

"Maybe we should go talk with Snake, with his leg up in traction maybe he'll be more cooperative."

"And maybe he won't. Maybe he'll lie just as effortlessly and tell us the wrong thing to do," with that North grabbed his coat and hat.

"Where you going?"

"I don't know. Just for a walk; need to clear my head."

Of the four hundred daily commercial flights out of Chicago Midway, Lakeland was the destination, or a stop, for four of them. Jaeger checked the board, there were two remaining flights from Midway. The first, Eastern flight EA1227 scheduled to arrive at 5:25PM before continuing to Detroit and then onto Cleveland. The second was Continental flight CO823 scheduled to arrive at 7:45PM with Lakeland as its destination. There was also a private plane enroute from Meigs Field with an estimated arrival time of 5:00PM. He picked up the phone and called the tower, "John, what's the status on November One Zero Nine One Papa?"

"Well hello to you too, Harry," the flight controller responded sarcastically, "they're on our radar now, should be landing in ten minutes."

"Have it taxi to hanger one."

"Roger that!" the line went dead and Jaeger stood holding the handset for a moment before hanging up. He raced past Suzette in the lobby on his way to the hangers, "Are you leaving, Mr. Jaeger?" she asked.

"Mind your own business!" he snapped as he pushed the door open and stepped into the afternoon heat.

The plane taxied up to the hanger and the pilot cut the engine. Jaeger stepped under the wing as the pilot opened the door, "I'm Jaeger, you got something for me?"

The pilot gave him the once over as he stepped from the plane and grabbed a small valise from behind the seat, "What're you talking about, bub?"

"Weren't you given a package for me?" Jaeger said with a crack in his voice.

"I think you're mistaking me for someone else, friend."

"You're coming in from Meigs right?"

"You writing a book?"

"How's that?"

"What's with all the questions, I told you I have no idea what you're talking about, now get out of my way," with that the pilot locked the door to the plane, pushed his way past Jaeger and walked toward the terminal.

Jaeger took a moment and looked into the plane and not seeing anything, walked back to his office.

A half hour later he walked onto the tarmac just as the door dropped on the Eastern Airlines flight. He watched as the passengers deplaned and as their luggage was pulled from the hold in the rear of the plan. He walked up to the baggage handler as he tossed bags onto the cart, "Anything in there with my name on it?"

"No, haven't seen any packages that are staying here."

Jaeger watched the passengers as they walked into the terminal. He took a cigarette from his pocket and began pacing without bothering to light it.

The two hour wait for the Continental flight moved at glacial speed. He paced, he smoked, and he got progressively more agitated. Finally in his office, he reached into the file cabinet and grabbed the bottle of gin and a glass he kept there. He poured out a couple of fingers and tossed it back. He sat down in the chair and felt the flush come to his cheeks.

After what felt like a week had passed, he watched the landing lights of Continental CO823 as it made its approach over Lake Michigan and rushed down the runway. It turned onto the taxiway and made its way back to the terminal. He watched as the stairway was rolled up and passengers began to deplane. He walked to the tail as luggage was pulled from the hold; as the baggage handler retrieved the last item he gave Jaeger a shrug and shook his head. "What the hell," he thought to himself. He was walking past the passenger stair when someone called down to him.

"Is your name Harold?" asked a young blond stewardess.

Surprised, he turned on his heel, "Yeah, uh yes, I'm Harold, Harold Jaeger."

She began down the stairs, "I've got something for you," she said vacuously as she handed him a small vinyl bag with the Continental logo imprinted on its side. He took the bag and tried to look calm as he walked quickly to his office.

North stood looking out the squad room windows onto the street below. One by one, shops went dark as their owners headed to their dinners and their beds. Two cars of teens raced past the Safety Building only to be stopped by a police car that had just happen to pull from the lot as they sped by. North smiled and turned back to his desk; Davis' head, inches from the phone, rested on his arms. Tiffin broke the silence, "It's eight, I should be getting home." No sooner had he spoken when the phone rang and Davis shot straight upright.

North held a finger up, "Remember your part, Davis."

The young officer nodded his head and picked up the receiver, "Yeah?" he said brusquely.

"It's Jaeger. I'll have a package for you in the usual place."

"When?"

"By ten," the call ended and Davis replaced the receiver. "He says the package will be in the usual place by ten."

Tiffin patted him on the back, "Good job, Davis!"

"Thank you, Detective. You need my help with the, uh, package?"

North shook his head, "No, we've got it from here."

Davis nodded and headed for the stairs.

"I better call Kaye, it's going to be a late night." Tiffin dialed his number and spoke quietly to his wife.

"How'd she take the news?" North said with a grin on his face.

"She said her next husband won't be a cop."

Tiffin gassed the car at the city yard while North spread a map over the hood, "Look here," he said as he pointed his finger to a point on the map, "if we drive down Upton we can park about a five hundred feet from the back of the machine shop, we should be able to keep an eye on Jaeger and not be spotted."

"See those blue coveralls hanging over there?"

"Sure, what're you thinking?"

"I'm thinking that we can drape those over the headlights and bumper to avoid a reflection if he sweeps the area with a flashlight or something."

"That's the smartest thing you've said this evening," North joked. "Yeah, grab them."

They drove out Main to Territorial and worked their way behind the machine shop. North had been wrong about the distance, they were a mere football field length from the shed. He was able to pull behind some heavy brush but still had a good line of sight. Tiffin got out and threw the coveralls over the front of the car. Then they waited.

About ten after ten they saw a dark Mercury drive slowly by the shop. A couple of minutes later, the same car pulled into the lot and turned its headlights off. It drove toward the back of the building and sat there for a few minutes.

Tiffin strained to see through the darkness, "Can you see what he's doing?"

"As far as I can tell, he's just sitting there." At that moment the dome light of the car snapped on as the driver opened the door. Jaeger stepped out and walked around the car, stopping on each side to look around.

"Nervous, isn't he?" Tiffin whispered.

"With good reason."

After he had made certain the area was clear, he opened the trunk and pulled something out. He made his way to the shed and lifted the cover. He dropped the lid to the barrel as he pulled it off, which started dogs barking for a half mile radius. He carefully put the lid on, closed the cover, got into his car and drove off. It didn't look like he turned on the headlights until he was well down the road.

Tiffin nodded at his partner, "Ready?"

"Hold you horses, let's make sure he doesn't circle back or something."

They waited for thirty minutes before getting out of the car. The two then carefully crossed the vacant lot that separated their car from the machine shop. Tiffin kept watch as North quietly retrieved the package. Then as quickly as they could, they made their way back to the Mainline.

Tiffin removed the coveralls and North tossed the package into the glove compartment.

"How much does that weigh?" Tiffin asked as North backed out of the hideaway and onto the road.

"Maybe half a pound."

"What do you figure it's worth?"

North thought for a few moments, "Depending on how much it's cut, a year's pay, maybe more."

Tiffin gave a little whistle, "What's Jaeger going to do when he doesn't get paid?"

"That, my friend, is one of the unknowns in this plan."

# Chapter 15

It was after midnight by the time they had written their report and gotten the heroin checked into the evidence locker. Tiffin yawned and stretched, "That's enough for me, I don't have another ounce of energy left." He looked to his partner, "You going to call it a day?"

North sat and thought for a moment, "Yeah, there's nothing more to do tonight. Think I'll see Roxy for a nightcap." They grabbed their belongings and Tiffin turned off the switch which ceased the incessant humming of the fluorescent lights.

The Trophy Room was empty except for Roxy and Charlie when he walked in, "Too late for a drink?"

Charlie frowned, "To be honest, I was just thinking about locking up. What would you think about taking a bottle home with you?"

Brick nodded, "Works for me. Put it on my tab?"

The bar owner slid a bottle across the bar, "If it means we can close up, absolutely." North took it and walked the two blocks to the Swanson. Once in the room he got out of his clothes and sat up on the bed with a glass of bourbon in his hand. He sipped slowly and thought about the events of the past week. He got up, grabbed his worn leather notebook, sat down at the table and began writing.

Denslow: where did she die?

Dalander: who killed/why?

De Luca: why was he on me?

Como: Implicate? Make it stick?

He picked up the glass and sipped as he rolled the questions around in his mind. "Denslow died of an overdose," he thought, "but she didn't die in the airplane or here. Where did that happen? Did De Luca kill Dalander and who pointed me out to De Luca in the first place?" That last question bothered him most at the moment. Within three hours of finding Denslow, Como's goon was on him.

"Jaeger!" he said aloud. The airport manager was the only logical explanation. Comfortable with that knowledge he turned off the light and lay down on the bed. Much needed sleep followed.

Nearby thunder awakened both North and the memories of the battle at Monte Cassino. His heart raced and he had to consciously slow his breathing. "Damn!" He swung his legs off the bed and looked out the window into a rolling thunderstorm. A flash of lightening followed immediately by the crash of thunder caused him to jump. North opened the bottle of bourbon and took a swig. As he slowly woke the shaking stopped.

He looked at his watch and saw that it was almost seven. He grabbed his kit and went to the bathroom.

Thirty minutes later he walked down Main, ducking under awnings and overhangs when he could. By the time he stepped into the Fifth Wheel his socks were saturated. Shaking the rain off the Bradmore he put it on the stool next to him.

"Coffee?" a young waitress asked.

As he reached out to take the offered cup he heard the bell over the door tinkle. "Thought you might be here," Tiffin said as he put his umbrella in the corner. "What did you eat yesterday?"

"Didn't we have lunch?"

"No," Tiffin said as he motioned for the waitress to bring him a cup, "I had lunch and you watched." The waitress brought him a cup, "Shoot me some cream and sugar and we'll both have corned beef hash and a couple of poached eggs."

"I hate poached eggs and, if you hadn't noticed, you're not my mother."

"Kaye's worried about you; therefore I'm worried by association."

North called after the waitress, "Make mine over hard."

As they ate, North caught his partner up on his thoughts. "You're right, only Jaeger could have notified De Luca. But, what," Tiffin paused as he slid a forkful into his mouth, "what was De Luca doing here in the first place?"

"His calendar indicated that he was going to meet Dalander at the airport. But you're right, why? If Dalander picked up his drugs in Chicago, why the detour?"

"Maybe he was short changing Como and Como didn't want blood on his doorstep?" Tiffin thought out loud.

A forkful of hash hovered in front of North's mouth before he put the fork down on his plate, "De Luca had a pound of heroin in his car, he must have been bringing it to Dalander to distribute."

191

"What about the cash he had with him? Not many people carry a thousand dollars around with them."

"Maybe he left some drugs somewhere else between Skokie and here. He was in Niles, that's only a few miles up from South Bend, maybe he had a distributor serving Notre Dame."

Tiffin gave North a quizzical look, "Hard to believe kids at Notre Dame would be using heroin."

"Why, because they're Catholic or because they come from money?"

"You're right; kids will do anything if someone tells them that it's fun."

"Or will help them study."

"Or be popular," Tiffin added.

"Exactly, they're easily duped into trying anything." North picked his fork up again and ate the bite of hash, "And as easy as it is to get hooked on heroin, they become steady customers."

The rain had let up by the time they finished breakfast and they walked through the fresh cool air to the Safety Building. Inside and up the stairs, North put his moist fedora on the coat rack and draped his coat on his chair. Tiffin looked across the desk, "When do you think we should let Jaeger know to go look for the money?"

"He's gotta be nervous, so let him stew in his own juices for a bit; late tonight, maybe."

They caught the Chief up on their progress and Brick called Memorial Hospital. A perky voice answered, "Doctor Howard's office."

"Detective North for the Doc."

"I'm sorry, sir; Doctor Howard on rounds. May I ask him to return your call?"

North rubbed his temples with his free hand, "Yes."

"May I ask as to what this is pertaining?"

"He'll know."

"May I have your phone number?"

North grew irritated, "He'll know that too!" he shouted into the receiver as he slammed it down. Others in the squad room looked his way for a moment before going back to their work.

"Hey, partner. Syl's going to be alright," Tiffin offered.

"You don't know that."

"I've got faith."

North shot Tiffin an infuriated look and lowered his voice, "The only thing I believe is that Como is about to lose his luck, and if Syl doesn't come around, he just might lose his life."

Jaeger anxiously paced his office. He'd never arranged a deal before nor had he ever been on the hook; at least not like this. Drugs came in, cash came back and he took his cut. It was simple and he felt safe, at least as long as he didn't double-cross Como. But this time it was different, this time he'd made a deal with the devil and put not only his own life, but his boy's lives on the line. "He wouldn't hurt my kids," he tried to convince himself without much luck. Nine-thirty in the morning didn't seem too early for a drink.

The phone on North's desk rang, "Michigan Bell, what number are you calling? Uh-huh, no, that number is out of order at the moment."

Tiffin gave him a quizzical look, "How long do you think we can keep this up before someone tells Mrs. Nelson her line isn't dead?"

"Hopefully longer than we need to use her line."

The Chief walked toward his detectives, "Just spoke to the Fire Chief, he's onboard."

"Weird, huh?" Tiffin asked.

"How's that?" the Chief replied.

"Us asking them for help."

Cummings turned and walked back toward his office. He stopped and looked over his shoulder, "Yeah, and I'm going to hear about it for years. Just make sure this works."

North gave him a nod, "We'll do our best."

"You better do better than that!" the glass in the Chief's door rattled as he slammed it shut.

The detectives were talking over some details when Tiffin's phone rang, "Detective Tiffin, oh hey Doc, here's Brick."

North took the receiver, "How's Syl?"

"She's still posturing but it's relaxing. She looks better than she did yesterday."

"That's good, right?"

"I don't want to get your hopes up, but it may be indicative of some brain function. I did insert a feeding tube today; trying to give her every chance possible."

"Thanks for the update," and he handed the receiver back to Tiffin.

"Good news?"

North sat, "Sounds like the same news said in different words. Let's get to work."

Throughout the morning and into the afternoon the two made a number of phone calls and met with members of the department. Plans finalized, Tiffin left to see his son play a little league game and spend some time with his family before he returned to work what might be another late night. North took a walk to Turner's Smoke Shop. A small bell tinkled when he pushed the screen door open.

The shopkeeper looked up from behind the counter, "Good afternoon, Mr. North. What can I get you today?"

"A carton of Pall Malls and a few boxes of matches."

Turner grabbed the red carton of cigarettes and slid it into a narrow bag. He tossed four small boxes of wooden matches into the bag, "You lose your Zippo?"

North counted out one dollar and eighty five cents from his coin purse, "No, just needed some matches." Turner pressed the right keys on the cash register and the till popped open.

"Alright then Mr. North, see you soon," the shopkeeper said as Brick pulled the screen door in causing the bell to tinkle again.

Back at the Swanson he stopped at the front desk and spoke with the manager for a moment before heading up to the third floor. Once in the room he kicked his shoes off, hung the holster on the back of the chair and, propping himself up, stretched out on the bed. He took the Colt, swung the cylinder away from the frame and gave it a spin before he clicked it back into place and put it on the bedspread next to his right thigh.

A knock on his door woke him from a nap he had not expected to take, "It's seven o'clock," a voice said through the door.

"Thanks Mike," North muttered through a very dry mouth. He got his shoes, holster and jacket back on, grabbed the Bradmore and locked the door behind himself. In the lobby he climbed up onto the shoeshine stand and nodded to the kid behind the sundry stand.

"I hope you don't mind me saying so…" the youth began.

North offered a wry smile, "Yeah, I know; I'm hard on my shoes."

He and Tiffin arrived at the steps of the Safety Building at about the same time. "Ready?" Tiffin asked.

North, recalling a phrase he heard in France during the war, smiled, "Le bon temps roule."

"Come again?"

"Let the good times roll!"

Tiffin laughed, "Oh like, 'Let the games begin?'"

"Yeah, like that."

In the squad room the Chief and a couple of other detectives were waiting; cigarette smoke filled the room. North took them in, "Where's Davis?" he asked.

Cummings said, "Sergeant Higdon tells me that Davis and Williamson caught a burglary in progress, they're booking our new house guest down in the cells."

Twenty minutes passed before they heard the elevator bell chime. Davis entered the room, "Am I late?" he said with a smile.

North shook his head, "How can you be late, the show doesn't start without you. Ready?"

"I looked at the notes, let's do this."

North dialed the phone and handed him the receiver, a breathy voice answered, "Lakeside Airport."

"Need me to talk to Jaeger," Davis said in his best ghetto voice.

"One moment please," came the breathy reply.

The phone was answered on the first ring, "Harold Jaeger."

"Jaeger, got you some cash if you want it." Everyone in the squad room held their breath.

A thankful tone came to Jaeger's voice, "Yes! When?"

"Eleven tonight. And if you see lights, keep driving, I don't want to look at your ugly white face." With that Davis slammed the phone down, "Hope you don't mind, I kinda made up that last part."

"No," Tiffin spoke for the audience, "that was perfect!"

By half past ten the Ford was once again carefully hidden in the bushes behind the tool and die shop. The sound of cicadas and crickets created a musical backdrop to the stakeout, "I wish we were close enough to see the look on Jaeger's face," Tiffin whispered.

North nodded, "I agree."

The two sat quietly for quite some time before a familiar dark Mercury drove slowly past the front of the shop on Territorial, "There's our boy," North observed.

Like before, Jaeger pulled a U-turn, turned his lights off and drove slowly down the side of the building, stopping near the shed. He got out of the car and carefully looked around. Satisfied that he was alone, he flicked on his flashlight and approached the shed. He carefully lifted the lid and used a stick to prop it up. He then pulled up the top of the drum and ever so quietly placed it atop the drum next to it.

The detectives could make out Jaeger reaching around inside the drum before he shone the light into it. In a panic, Jaeger pulled the crate out of the drum and tossed it aside, leaned in and inspected the inside with his flashlight. He then shined the light between the barrels and crawled on top of them to look between. In all, he spent about five minutes checking and rechecking before he hurriedly ran back to his car, started the engine and drove out.

"I think our Harold is upset," Tiffin said.

North pushed the starter, "Frightened is more like it."

Twenty minutes later the phone on North's desk began to ring. There was no one there to answer it.

Jaeger paced the floor of the shabby apartment he rented above the Fatsco Hardware store near downtown. Ten minutes after he first called Nelson's number, he called again, and again there was no answer. "Sonofabitch," he shouted as he slammed the phone down.

Over the course of the night, Jaeger paced, smoked and made calls to a phone that refused to be answered. He had never felt this kind of helplessness in his life. Panic rolled over him in waves that left him emotionally and physically exhausted. At six-thirty the sun rose and Jaeger tried the number again, and again there was no answer. Not knowing what else to do, he set the percolator to boil and washed up. Once he had washed the sweat off himself, he poured a cup of coffee, sat at the table and stared into the dark liquid. At eight the whistle blew at a nearby foundry that announced the start of the day shift; Jaeger pushed himself away from the table and poured the cup of coffee into the sink.

North walked over to the coffee urn and was pleasantly surprised to find coffee pour into his cup as he turned the handle.

Tiffin walked into the squad room and took off his hat and coat, "Morning Brick; you get any sleep last night?"

He took a sip of the coffee, "Probably more than Jaeger did." He took another sip of coffee, "Ready for the next step?"

"What did you say last night? 'Lay bonds tempt ruler.'"

North chuckled, "Let's see if Chicago PD has given us the right number." He picked up the receiver on Tiffin's desk, "Get me the Chicago operator."

"Right away, detective," a pleasant female voice replied.

"Operator."

"I need to call Skokie, Fairfax 9-9675."

"It's ringing now," the operator said before she signed off the call.

A woman with a tired voice answered, "Como residence."

"Listen carefully, doll. Tell Como that Jaeger in LaSalle Harbor won't be able to pay him." In the background he heard a familiar voice ask, "Who's on the phone?"

"I don't know; someone who says that Jaeger won't be paying."

North hung up as Como said, "What do you mean he…"

The phone in the airport manager's office was on its fourth ring before it was answered, "Harold Jaeger."

"Jaeger! I got a call that said you won't be paying me, what the hell's up with that?"

"Mr. Como? Uh, who called and said that?"

"I'm askin' the questions; understand?"

"Of course I understa…"

"Am I going to get paid or not?"

Jaeger's guts twisted themselves into a knot, "Of course you're going to get paid."

There was a long enough silence that Jaeger began to wonder if they had been disconnected, "When?" Como finally asked.

"When?" Jaeger repeated.

"What are you, a fuckin' myna bird? When am I going to get the money you owe me?"

Jaeger's mind raced for an answer, "Uh, I was told I'll have it by tonight."

"Good, then you'll have fifty-five hundred dollars all wrapped up for me tomorrow."

"Fifty-five hundred?" Jaeger stammered.

"You remember that I said I'd set the price? That's the price." There was a click that told Jaeger that the call had ended.

He turned to the credenza and fumbled in his pocket for a key. With shaking hands, he unlocked the right side of the credenza and pulled out a metal box which he placed on his desk. He fumbled with the keys again and managed to get the box open and counted the cash it held; cash which represented everything he'd earned in his business partnership with Como. "Twenty seven hundred and forty two." He tossed the money into the box and threw the box back into the credenza. "Shit," he said to himself as he reached into the file cabinet for the gin.

A breathy voice answered the phone, "Lakeland Airport."

"How's your boss this morning?" North asked cheekily.

Suzette lowered her voice to a conspiratorial level, "Brick! He stormed in, flew past me and I heard the door to his office slam. That was thirty minutes ago, I haven't seen or heard from him since."

"Listen doll, things are going to be coming to a head. This is what I need you to do," North described the next step in his plan, "Can you do that?"

"I think I can get it done."

North ended their call, "Okay, thanks. Talk to you soon." Suzette hung up the phone, picked up the receiver and dialed an outside number.

Cummings exited his office and walked to where North and Tiffin were seated, "I just got off the horn with the DA; he says we either charge your Mr. Henry or let him go."

Infuriated, North turned toward his boss, "If we cut him loose we can kiss this plan goodbye."

The chief nodded thoughtfully and turned on his heel, "Dammit, I get so frustrated with the way the paperwork gets misplaced around here."

Tiffin looked at his partner, "What does that mean?"

"That means," North smiled, "that he bought us a day or so."

By noon, a crew was busy laying bales of straw along the shoulders of the entry road to the airport. Inquisitive, one of the baggage handlers wandered into the terminal, "Hey Suzette, what's with the straw?"

"County said they will be planting some grass seed along the road and the straw will keep the moisture in," Suzette replied. "You better get outside, Continental out of Detroit is inbound and will be landing any moment."

The baggage handler tipped his campaign hat toward Suzette and strolled back onto the tarmac.

North grabbed up the keys to the Mainline and went first to Talbot's Drug Store then to Gillespie's Drugs. In both businesses he purchased all the Epsom salt and rubbing alcohol they had. Old man Gillespie questioned the detective who answered only, "Home remedy," as he left with his packages. At the hardware store he bought a dozen galvanized steel buckets before returning to the Safety Building.

Tiffin helped carry the purchases which they put into a first floor storage room. "You sure this is going to work?"

"The chemistry will work, if that's what you mean."

"What about the plan?"

"Too many things can go wrong; let's concentrate on the things we know we can do right."

Tiffin, smiled as he remembered the new phrase he learned, "Ah, lay bonds tempt ruler."

"Le bons temps roule!" North corrected.

"Isn't that what I just said?" There was irritation in Tiffin's voice.

"Close enough."

They walked through the plan with the chief and with Higdon who would supply the necessary uniformed officers. Lou tidied up the holding cells in case they had unexpected visitors. In all, there was heightened anticipation among the entire department, even though only a few knew about the plan, which, like in any police department, meant that pretty much everyone knew about it.

Jaeger grabbed the package of cigarettes from his desk at the exact moment he remembered that he smoked the last one. He dug around in his pockets, came up with thirty cents and wandered to the cigarette machine in the lobby. He dropped in the quarter and nickel and pulled the lever; a pack of smokes and a book of matches slid into the tray at the bottom of the machine.

"You okay, Mr. Jaeger," Suzette called after him, "I haven't seen you all day."

"Just do your job and leave me alone," he shouted over his shoulder as he walked down the corridor to his office. Suzette heard the door slam. As afternoon turned to evening she watched the sun set into Lake Michigan. After having gotten the last passenger onto the last scheduled flight of the night, she turned off the lights at the ticket counter and left the building.

Back at her apartment, she called the number on Brick's card, "LaSalle Harbor police,"

"Connect me to Detective North."

"Please hold," the line momentarily went dead followed by the soft purr of a ringing phone heard over the line.

"Detective Tiffin."

"Is Brick, er Detective North there?"

"One moment," Tiffin cupped his hand over the mouthpiece, "It's Suzette."

North grabbed the receiver, "What do you need, doll?"

"I just wanted you to know that everything is in place." He handed the receiver back to Tiffin who put it on the cradle.

As they left the squad room, Tiffin turned, "What makes you so sure that Como will come here?"

"So far, he's lost about a pound and a half of heroin, a thousand dollars in cash, and one of his henchmen. And now, Jaeger isn't going to cough up a bunch of money. I don't think Como will send a lieutenant to clean this up; he'll want to fix it himself."

Anxious, Tiffin responded, "I hope you're right."

North turned and stopped on his way down the stairs to the lobby, "I hope I'm right too." Once outside he loosened his tie and took a walk. Within ten minutes he was walking along the bluff looking out over Lake Michigan. He watched as a sailboat tacked against the wind and made its way into the harbor and the yacht club. As he sat on a bench, he sensed someone approaching from behind, he stood and spun, his hand on the handle of the Colt.

"Mind if I sit with you?" Suzette said as she walked up.

Surprised, he pointed to the bench, "Sit down. What're you doing here?"

She glanced over her left shoulder, "It's just a few blocks to my apartment; I come down here a lot in the evenings, get some fresh air and sometimes stop for an ice cream. I've never seen you here before."

"I just walked in a different direction tonight. Normally my walks keep me close to Main Street."

"How fortunate for me! Want some ice cream?"

"I don't think so, doll."

She cocked her head and said in a playful tone, "Then walk with me while I go get a cone?" North nodded and stood up, Suzette took his arm, "I feel safer like this," she smiled and put her head on his shoulder.

The two walked down State Street and Suzette paused and looked into the windows of dress shops and department stores, occasionally pointing something out. North relaxed for a moment, perhaps for the first time since Sylvia was kidnapped. His mind began to race; he wanted this woman, at least for this night to help him forget about the past week, but the connection he felt to Sylvia was an emotion that he'd never truly experienced before.

At the ice cream shop he purchased her a cone, "Oh, this is good," she said as she pushed the cone toward him, "try it." The cone brushed against his lips. She looked up at him, "Here, let me clean that up," she said as she put her arms around him and kissed the ice cream off his lips. Her kiss was warm and sensual, his response was cold.

Suzette's feminine intuition sprang into life, "Who is she?" she asked without a hint of resentment.

"A woman who I put into harm's way."

"You have feelings for her, don't you?

"I have feelings that I've never had before for a woman."

She looked up at North, "If it doesn't work out, remember that I have those same kind of feelings for you, Brick." She gave him another kiss, this one on the cheek, and quietly walked away toward Colfax Avenue. North stood and watched her go.

He walked back to the Swanson and had a couple of shots of bourbon before he fell into a restless sleep. In his dreams, sexual images of Suzette in bed were replaced in his mind's eye of Sylvia in her hospital bed.

Jaeger tried Nelson's number half a dozen times as he wore a path in the linoleum, "I'll give Como the money I have and work off the rest," he thought. "I'll promise to pay him interest; he's a business man, he'll go for that." The thoughts didn't bring him relief, nor did the gin that he liberally poured.

Sunrise was six-thirty; North was already up and at the Fifth Wheel, the Palladium spread out on the empty counter. He read that Viet Cong Guerrillas bombed and assassinated more than 400 South Vietnamese officials in Saigon. "The world doesn't learn," he muttered to himself. Turning to the sports page he read that Mickey Mantle hit his two hundredth career home run. He used the end of a piece of toast to wipe the bacon grease off his plate, swallowed the last bit of coffee in his cup, left three half-dollars on the counter, and walked toward the Safety Building.

He, Tiffin and the uniforms assigned to him, waited in the squad room. Conversations were at a minimum, most everyone kept an eye on the telephone on Tiffin's desk. The hours slowly passed. Chief Cummings came in, leaned against a table, tamped the ashes down in his pipe, and exhaled the fragrant smoke, "Maybe we can get these guys on the street until you need them."

As if on cue, Tiffin's phone rang. North was first to it, "Detective North."

"Brick, five minutes ago I put a call through to Jaeger."

"Did you catch who called?"

"I listened in."

"Even better," North smiled, "so who was it?"

"I don't know, but he told Jaeger he'd be here at sundown and Jaeger better have his money."

"That's got to be our guy. Did he say whether he was flying in or driving?"

"Sorry, he didn't, just that he'd be here at sunset."

"Thanks, I owe you."

There was a pause before Suzette said, "What I want, you won't give me." The line went dead.

North replaced the receiver, "Okay. Sunset at the airport."

Cummings looked at his men, "Be back here by six and ready to go."

The day seemed to drag. North got the buckets out of the closet and poured several pounds of Epson salt into each. With each bucket he placed a quart of rubbing alcohol. At midday he drove over to the hospital and rode up to the fourth floor. The smell of cleaning solutions met the elevator, "I'm here to see Miss Kingston," he said to the nurse as he walked past her. No one tried to stop him from doing so.

Sylvia's eyes were open and for a moment his heart soared, "Syl!" There was no response, just a blank stare. He saw that her arms were at her sides, but her hands were clenched in fists. The IV tube still ran to her collarbone and he saw a tube in her nose which he guessed was the feeding tube Howard had told him about.

"Oh, Syl," he said softly. He sat on the chair next to her for a few minutes before he stood up, leaned over, and kissed her on the forehead.

A couple of officers took the buckets to the airport and put them strategically near the bales of hay that had been placed the day before. Brown glass bottles of rubbing alcohol were laid near the buckets before the officers retreated.

By eight, North and Tiffin were in the terminal; just a couple of travelers. Four officers were hidden in a hanger waiting with their black and white police cars. Four additional officers were hidden along the entry road, each with a box of matches.

At eight forty-five, a black Cadillac Series 75 limousine pulled down the airport road. In addition to the driver, there was another person in the front seat. In the rear compartment, behind the glass, was a large man and a platinum blonde. The Caddie stopped in front of the terminal and the front seat passenger jumped out and opened the back door of the car. The blonde stepped out followed by Como, a homburg hat on his head. He walked with authority into the Terminal, the blonde on his heel. Suzette looked up from the counter, "May I help you, sir?"

"Where can I find Jaeger?"

"Let me call him for you," she said with a smile.

"Just tell me where he is, I'll surprise him."

Connie took Como's arm, "I'll show you where he is," and she led him toward the back of the Terminal. Looking back to the ticket counter, she smiled and in an antagonistic tone, said, "Hello, Suzette."

As Como and Connie turned down the corridor, the driver and passenger entered the lobby and looked directly at North and Tiffin. "Why don't you two take a hike," the passenger said toward the detectives.

North chuckled at the two, "Yeah, that's not going to happen." At that, two of the officers entered the terminal, their guns drawn on Como's goons. North and Tiffin drew their weapons and pointed them at their adversaries who were handcuffed and taken to the hanger where the other officers waited. Once they were away from the terminal, North had Suzette switch the outdoor terminal lights off and on twice.

The officers down the entry road saw the lights blink, placed the buckets on top of bales of hay and proceeded to pour the rubbing alcohol into them. Once the alcohol was in each, they went back down the road and dropped a lit match into each. The salt and alcohol burst into eight foot flames. With poles, the four officers pushed the buckets over which poured the burning liquid onto the dry straw which instantly caught fire. Flames reached toward the sky along the length of the entrance road, the orange glow caught the Connie's attention inside Jaeger's office.

Como had Jaeger's back against the wall opposite the window, "We had a deal and that deal wasn't for half the money."

"Fire!" Connie yelled, "There's a fire out there!"

Jaeger tried to push past the mobster, "I've got to call the fire department!"

"Fuck the fire! You've got bigger things to worry about."

On cue, Suzette screamed down the corridor, "Fire! We've got a fire!" before she ducked behind the ticket counter.

Connie grabbed at Como's arm, "Alberto, we need to go."

"Not until I make this idiot understand that no one fucks with Lucky Como," he fired one shot which struck the sweating airport manager in the throat. Gurgling and clawing at his neck, Jaeger slid to the ground. Como took the money off the desk and made his way down the corridor and into the terminal. North and Tiffin were waiting for him with their guns drawn.

"Drop the gun, Como," North barked.

"I know this voice," he said as he looked at North, "you're the asshole that said, how did you put it? 'You better hope you find me before I find you.' Well, looks like I found you first." Como lifted the .45 he was carrying and pulled Connie in front of himself as a shield. He pointed the weapon toward North.

Tiffin, thinking he had a clean shot, fired one round which passed through Connie and grazed Como's side. Como dropped Connie and fired, striking Tiffin in the chest. Tiffin's gun skittered across the floor.

North took his attention off Como just long enough to see Tiffin crumple to the floor. In that moment, Como swung his gun toward North and fired, hitting him near the scar on his right side. Pain ripped through his consciousness and for a moment he was back in Monte Cassino, the sound of planes and bombs and children screaming filled his mind. North fell to his knees as Como walked up and placed the .45 against the detective's head, "Fucking cops, you're all too stupid to learn that your luck will always run out before mine does."

Como's voice brought North back to the moment; he grimaced through the pain, "Go ahead, kill me. But first, I need to know what happened to Dalander."

"Dalander? Fucking Swede was skimming heroin from each package and, shorting me on payments. I sent De Luca to take care of the problem."

"What about Dalander's girl?"

"That whore? Guess she shot up too much, too often, on my drugs and finally overdosed. Dalander brought her with him thinking we'd clean up his mess. De Luca dumped her here for Jaeger to take care of; lazy bastard didn't get here quick enough."

"So why send De Luca after me?"

"You ask a lot of questions for a dead man."

He grimaced, "Humor me."

"I've learnt that most cops can be bought, the rest have to be gotten rid of in other ways. Needed to know which you was."

"So why kill Jaeger?"

Como pressed the gun into North's forehead, "Shut up, I'm done talking."

The gunshot echoed through the building. North knelt there, surprised he was alive. He looked up at Como whose eyes were wide with disbelief; blood spurted from his mouth as he fell to the ground. With the mobster out of his line of vision, he saw Suzette holding Tiffin's revolver, its barrel still pointing where Como's head had been seconds before. North pushed himself up to his feet and took the gun from her hands as uniformed officers rushed through the entrance.

North turned and saw his partner's body on the tile floor, blood spreading from an exit wound hidden behind his back, "Barry!" he shouted as he crouched down next to Tiffin's still form.

"Did you just call me by my first name?" Tiffin asked in a weak voice.

# EPILOGUE

The LaSalle Harbor Fire Department already had the fires doused as two ambulances raced from the airport toward Memorial Hospital. Once there, orderlies ran up to the cars and pulled the doors open; North saw a familiar face, "Wilson, James Wilson!"

"Detective?!"

"Take care of my partner first, he's in the other ambulance; I'm not in bad shape."

"Yes, sir!" Wilson ran to the other ambulance and, with another orderly's help, got Tiffin's gurney into the Emergency Room entrance.

"Are you always a nice guy?" Connie asked.

"Normally," North replied to the woman strapped to the gurney next to his.

She gave a reflective smile, "I never had any luck with nice guys."

The orderlies rolled North into the emergency room, cut away his shirt and took him to the X-ray department. He was then taken back to the examination room, where he waited what seemed like hours. His mind occasionally drifting back to memories of Italy and the friends he left on the battlefield.

During one of those journeys of memory, Doc Howard came in to the exam room and held an X-ray up to the fluorescent lights.

North looked to his friend, "How's Tiff?"

"Out of surgery; lucky son of a bitch, bullet went through and managed to miss everything important. It did fracture his scapula, though. He'll recover quickly enough."

He probed North's wound with his finger, while the detective gritted his teeth, "The good news is that the rib was already broken and the bullet exited your side. The bad news is that I'm going to have to go in and remove some bone fragments."

"Won't be the first piece of rib someone has pulled out of my side. Should be a couple of women made out of those like in that Bible story."

"Well, I think there's a woman here for you now, you want to see her before I take you to surgery."

North nodded and the curtain parted, Suzette walked in, "Just wanted to make sure my favorite detective is alright."

"I'm fine, doll. Thanks to you."

She leaned over the gurney, pushed his mop of hair back and gave him a kiss on the forehead, "Remember, there's someone out there who loves you." With that, she turned and left; North watched her hips sway to her heel-to-toe gait.

Minutes later Wilson and another orderly rolled North up to the operating room where they slid him onto the table. A couple of nurses carefully washed and disinfected the area around the wound and draped surgical cloths over his torso. The anesthesiologist came in, introduced himself and placed a mask over his face, "Just count backward from one hundred."

North complied, "One hundred, ninety-nine, ninety-eight, ninety-seven, ninety…"

He woke in a semi-private room, the curtain pulled between himself and his roommate. Chief Cummings was sitting in a chair, puffing at his pipe. "North, you're awake! Good. Mel says you came through surgery just fine. They'll release you later today."

"Mel?" North questioned through a dry mouth.

"Doc Howard; wait, you don't know his first name?"

"Never asked," North said as he took in his surroundings. He noticed the sun was up and looked at the curtain that separated the beds, "Who's my roommate?"

Cummings stood and pulled back the curtain to reveal Tiffin asleep in the bed, Kaye at his side, "I should be mad at you for almost getting Barry killed," she said. "But I'm just glad you two are alive."

North nodded in her direction, not knowing what to say.

There was a knock at the door and Chief Cummings rose to answer it. Doc Howard poked his head in, "Don't want to disturb you. How are you feeling?"

"I'm good."

"There's someone out here who wants to see you."

North slowly shook his head, he really didn't want to see Suzette, but answered "Okay, bring her in."

The door opened fully and Doc Howard wheeled Sylvia into the room and up to the side of his bed. She reached out and put her hand on his arm and pulled herself up as close to his ear as she could, "I love you, too," she whispered.

## "Murder Unholy"
## A Brick North Mystery

Coming Fall 2020. In the small lakeside town of LaSalle Harbor members of the clergy are being killed. Why clergymen and what's the connection between a Catholic priest, a Jewish rabbi and a Baptist minister that could lead someone to kill them? North and Tiffin are swept up in intrigue and religious zealotry in this $2^{nd}$ volume of Brick North Mysteries.

Made in the USA
Middletown, DE
29 July 2020